SECRETS AND LIVES

SECRETS and LIVES

MARILYN FREEMAN

Spellbrooktales

Copyright

ISBN: 978-8384260-6-4

Contents

Chapter 1

SANDYLANDS

May 1972

The taxi pulled up in front of Sandylands. Joan paid the taxi driver, and he took her suitcase out of the boot. Glancing at her 'condition' he offered to carry her luggage into the nursing home for her. Joan declined his help saying that she could manage, thank you all the same. She hated the way people seemed to assume that to be pregnant meant being disabled in some way.

She stood for a moment or two as the taxi pulled away and then turned to look at the building that would be her home for the next three months. It was quite an imposing place, or at least it had been, once upon a time. She judged it was a couple of hundred years old and had been built as a private home. The notice at the end of the drive had just read 'Sandylands', with no hint of its current purpose. I suppose they have to be discreet about that, Joan thought. It wouldn't do to publicise that it was a place where unmarried mothers could come to give birth to their babies, 'out of wedlock', which was the polite, if old fashioned, way of putting it. She had long since realised that her current situation was viewed as something to be ashamed of, particularly for the woman, as though no man had actually been involved in its creation.

In her case, the man was long gone. She had thought he was the love of her life but once she gave him the news, he ran for the hills. Terrified she would tell his wife he severed all communication with her, and she realised what a fool she'd been. Well, she would have to live with the consequences. She was reading English at Manchester University and living in a bedsit with two other girls when she discovered she was pregnant. Her family home was in Bristol, but her parents were in Hong Kong. Her father was in the Diplomatic Corps and had been given a two-year posting just last year. She had wondered whether to tell them about the pregnancy, but in the end, as she had decided to have the baby adopted when it was born, she felt it best they didn't know anything about it. She was afraid they would try to persuade her to keep it, but she knew she wasn't ready to bring up a child on her own. There would be no help forthcoming from the father. Quite honestly, she felt she wouldn't want to bring up a child of his, given the irresponsible coward he had turned out to be.

Sandylands seemed a sensible choice as a place to have the baby. It was a private home and was rather expensive, but she had inherited some money from her grandmother, who would probably not have approved of the way she was spending it. However, she had little choice if she wanted to get her life back on track. She had come here straight from Manchester to have the baby, which would be adopted within a few weeks. She intended go home to Bristol afterwards and no one would be any the wiser. She would return to Manchester for the Autumn term to finish her degree.

As she entered the front door of Sandylands, a rather matronly figure approached her. She wore a nurse's uniform and cap and her bearing told Joan that she was definitely in charge here.

'Good afternoon, Miss Simons, I assume?' she said, stretching out her hand, 'I am Sister James.'

'Good afternoon,' Joan replied, shaking her hand.

'There are just a few formalities to attend to before we settle you in. Perhaps you would come into the office? Please leave your suitcase here for now, I'll find someone to help you with it later.'

Joan thanked her and followed her into an office next to the reception desk. Sister James installed herself in the chair at the far side of the desk and asked Joan to sit down opposite her. She took a form out of the desk and proceeded to ask Joan the usual questions. Full name, date of birth, religion, next of kin, home address. Not wishing there to be any connection between this place and her Bristol home, she gave the address of the flat in Manchester. Sister James then asked about her general health and well-being. Nothing to report there. Finally, she wanted to know whether her pregnancy so far had had any complications and had she been given a date for the birth of the baby. Joan assured her that so far all had gone well and it was due on the 24$^{th\ of}$ May. She was then asked to check the information on the form and sign and date it.

'Excellent!' declared Sister James. 'We'll get you settled in today and tomorrow we will give you a thorough examination and discuss arrangements for the birth of your baby, and what will follow.' As she followed Sister James back into reception, Joan thought, I know 'what will follow'. I hope they don't intend to try to persuade me to keep it.

A young man came forward and Sister James asked him to accompany Joan to Ward One and to carry her suitcase for her. She followed him up to the first floor, along the landing and through the door at the end. Joan didn't know what she expected, but the room didn't look like a hospital ward; more like a small dormitory in the girls' school she had attended by virtue of her father working overseas for the government. There were six beds, each with a small chest of drawers at one side and an armchair at the other. The occupants, unsurprisingly, were all young women in the latter stages of pregnancy. A couple of them were chatting to each other, one was busy knitting a baby cardigan and the others were reading. As Joan entered, they looked up briefly, nodded, and then went back to what they were doing. The nurse in attendance came forward, and with a friendly smile, took Joan's suitcase from the young man and led her to a bed at the far end of the room. Joan was rather put out that she would have to be sharing a room, she had hoped that, given the fees the place was charging, she would have had a room of her own. Oh well, she thought, after all, it wasn't meant to be a holiday, and set about unpacking her suitcase, resigned to being 'one of the girls' for a few weeks. Maybe once the baby was born, she would be given more privacy.

Actually, she settled in quite well. The 'girls' were more or less in the same position as she was, and they all had a lot in common. Safe to say, their opinion of the male sex was fairly uniformly poor, as they had all, in one way or another, been abandoned by the fathers of their babies. Their meals were eaten together in the dining room with other residents, some of whom had already had their babies and were staying with them for a few weeks, until they were either ready to take them home, or adoptions could be arranged for them.

Understandably, given the traumatic nature of what they were all going through, emotions were running high. Most of the girls, when the time came to give up their babies, were very upset, some of them inconsolable. Every few days a car would pull up outside the home and if a pregnant woman didn't get out, everyone knew that it meant a baby would be leaving its birth mother forever. Hearing the sobs, or sometimes even the heart wrenching wailing, of the mother as the child was taken away, was truly distressing and as the days and weeks passed, Joan wondered how she was going to feel when the time came. Before coming here, she had felt it wouldn't be difficult to give up her child because she had reasoned that it would be the best thing for them both. Now she realised that this wasn't about reasoning, or even just about emotion. It was about something much deeper; that visceral connection between a mother and her child, which after all, had literally been part of her body for months.

Physically, her pregnancy progressed well, and her body was almost ready to give birth. Emotionally, she wasn't so sure. How would she cope with the separation from her baby? Her due date came and went without any occurrence but two days later on 26th May, as she stood up from the dining table at breakfast time, her waters broke, and her contractions began. For a first labour, it was fairly short and with plenty of gas and air, the pain was bearable. The baby was born at eight o'clock that evening. He was a healthy boy, weighing eight pounds two ounces. She called him Peter, after her father.

In spite of her matter-of-fact attitude to giving up the baby, her body had different ideas. She wasn't prepared for the emotions this tiny bundle aroused in her. It consumed her. She just wanted to hold him. Breastfeeding him was unlike anything she had ever experienced. When he suckled her, it was as though he was still part of her, creating a sensation of intense pleasure that ran right down to the pit of her stomach. He was a lovely baby, perfect in every way, with dark hair and blue eyes, and none of the crumpled look some of the new-born babies had.

With each day that passed she loved him more and began to dread the day she would have to give him up. At the end of four weeks, she was asked to go to the office to speak to Sister James. It was with some apprehension that she knocked on the door. When she entered, Sister James was sitting at her desk and asked Joan to sit down in the chair opposite.

'We need to discuss what is going to happen to Peter,' Sister James said in a matter-of-fact tone.

'I know,' Joan replied.

'Do you still wish him to be adopted?' Sister James asked her quietly.

Joan paused, quite unable to answer for the moment. She knew what she would have to say, but the words wouldn't come.

'Take your time,' Sister James told her, 'I know it's a huge decision.'

Joan thought about her parents, her degree, her future that she had always imagined she would have, and the other future she and Peter would have as a single mother and her child in a world ill equipped or unable to help them.

Finally, she said,

'Yes, I want to have him adopted.'

'Very well then,' said Sister James. She paused and

then went on, 'Well, actually, we do have some people in mind. They are a nice couple who are unable to have their own child. I think they would suit Peter very well and give him a good home with a bright future ahead of him.'

So it was, that after four more weeks of looking after Peter, loving him, feeding him, bathing, and clothing him, Joan had to start to prepare to lose him. They made her wean him off the breast which broke her heart, but she knew it had to be done. He would have to be used to the bottle by the time she handed him over.

Sandylands had a policy of photographing the babies who were being adopted. Thoughtfully, they made sure their mothers had a copy. Over the next couple of weeks Joan gathered together a few of Peter's first clothes, placing them carefully in the front compartment of her suitcase along with his photo. Later, she would store them all safely in a box, which she would keep as the only permanent record of Peter's existence.

Finally, the day came, and the moment of separation arrived. One second, she was holding him, the next, Sister James had taken hold of him and left the room. Every fibre of Joan's being was crying out for her child. The physical pain she felt was horrendous and she broke down in tears as she had seen so many do before her.

She stayed a further three days at Sandylands before leaving for Bristol. She grieved for little Peter of course, but gradually the pain subsided and eventually she was ready to pick up the threads of her life again and return to Manchester to continue with her degree. Peter remained her secret, she never told anyone about him, not even her parents. When she went back to Manchester it was to a different flat and group of friends, and soon it was as though he had never existed. She blocked him out of her mind completely; well, almost.

Chapter 2

BRISTOL

2013

John West sat slouched in his rented room and eyed a brown stain of unknown origin on the carpet. The smell of cooking from one of the neighbours rooms seeped through the wall. He looked around the room and not for the first time, wondered how his life had come down to this. It was supposed to be furnished but a single bed, one chair, a small table, and a microwave next to the sink hardly justified the description. He'd bought a couple of things from the second-hand place round the corner, a rug, and an old armchair, which made it feel slightly more liveable, and his television, along with books from the charity shop gave him opportunities for escape from the grim reality of his life.

He had grown up in Bristol and always thought he had been born there, but when he was ten years old, his father, in one of his drunken rages had screamed at him that he wished they had never taken him in when his own mother didn't even want him. His world shifted. He was lost, and no matter how much his mother tried to reassure him that she loved him, he never quite believed it. His father's drinking got worse and eventually he disappeared from John's life. He simply left one day and never came home. After years of physical and mental abuse by him, particularly when he was drunk, John was relieved to see him go. He discovered later that his mother had thrown him out and he had joined the ranks of Bristol's homeless.

Shortly after his father disappeared, John and his mother had to leave their home, evicted for not paying the rent, and they moved into a tiny council flat. It was at the top of an eight-storey building and the lift hardly ever worked. There was damp and black mold around the windows and when the wind blew from the north it found its way in through the gaps where the window frames didn't fit properly.

John was actually a bright boy and had been doing well at school, until he had to change schools due to the move to a different area. He had always wanted to be a doctor but knew he would need to work hard to achieve that goal. He was sent to the local compre-hensive school which unfortunately didn't cater for children with such high-flying ambition. He did his best, but with no spare money for books, and hardly enough for decent clothes or even good food, he in-evitably found he was never quite good enough when it came to sitting exams. Living where they did it was difficult to find friends, apart from the ones in the local gangs. He resisted for as long as he could but eventually, out of sheer boredom and loneliness, he was drawn in.

Once in the gang he found that he was soon gaining the respect of the other members. He was intelligent and his particular forte was planning escapades, such as shoplifting, working out the best time to do the job and how to distract the shopkeeper whilst it was done. He didn't feel guilty about it. It felt good to be respected, and he felt he was entitled to have a few good things in life. It wasn't long before an older boy offered him the drugs. He tried to refuse but they told him if he wanted to belong to this gang, he must take them. After the first couple of times, he was hooked. He began stealing from wherever he could get the money to buy drugs, even from his mother when there was any spare around, which wasn't often. He was out of school more than he was in it. His whole nature changed, and he became angry and rude to his mother, showing her no respect whatsoever.

Eventually, the inevitable happened. He broke into a flat in the next block to find something to sell to feed his now well-established drugs habit. He was just sixteen years old. He chose the wrong flat and the man who lived there came home just as he was rifling through the drawers to see what he could find. The man grabbed him, and called the police. He was arrested, tried, and of course convicted of breaking and entering. On the advice of his solicitor, he asked for several other crimes to be considered and was found guilty on all counts. He was sent to a young offender's institution for two years, where he would be able to continue his education in criminal behaviour if he chose to do so. However, he made the decision that he would try to come off the drugs and hopefully to begin a new life when he left custody.

In fact, his luck did change on his release from prison. He was put in touch with a charity set up to help ex-offenders. His mother refused to have him back and he was found a room in a hostel. He was given a mentor, Alison Greaves, a middle-aged lady with sons of her own. Knowing that John had managed to break his drugs habit while in prison, and that he was a bright young man, she put a lot of effort into helping him to start afresh, managing to get him into a job working in a garden centre. After being cooped up in prison, John loved working outdoors and settled down to try to make a success of his life.

Everything seemed to be going fine until he noticed he was losing weight, which at first, he put down to working hard at the garden centre. However, one day when he woke up, he found that his vision was blurred. He had also noticed that he seemed thirsty all the time. When he mentioned all this to Alison, she suggested that he get checked out by his doctor. Her father had had similar symptoms and it turned out that he was diabetic. The doctor did some tests and diagnosed quite severe Type 1 diabetes, saying he would have to start using insulin by injecting himself every day. John was amazed, he hadn't really had any serious illnesses up to that point in his life and wasn't too pleased at the prospect of giving himself injections. Still, he reasoned, it has to be done, and he felt so much better once he had started treatment, that he accepted it as just something he would have to live with.

After a couple of years, he met Julie. She came to work at the garden centre and soon they were spending time together. Julie was also from Bristol but had had a better life than John. She knew about his history but admired the fact he was determined to make something of himself. He started to go to college part time, hoping to become a nurse. It would be a long road as he first had to gain some GCSE's as he had never completed any of them at school. He worked hard and after a couple of years had enough qualifications to apply for the Foundation Course.

He and Julie got engaged and moved into a two bedroomed flat in a nice area of Bristol. Life was good and John at last felt he might be able to put the past behind him. If he would never be a doctor, maybe he could be a nurse. In the meantime, once again with Alison's help as a referee, he was able to get a job working in the hospital as a nursing assistant on the grounds that he was studying for his qualifications.

He and Julie were married in the summer of '98 and it wasn't long before Julie announced she was pregnant. John was delighted. A child of his own! His own flesh and blood! Since finding out he had been adopted all those years ago, he had felt utterly alone in the world, without any real family of his own. He adored his little boy, James, and was a good dad, happy to share the caring with Julie.

About eighteen months later they had a little girl, Abigail. John was ecstatic, he had his family, he was making his way in the world. He felt that nothing could stop him now. Perhaps they may eventually even buy a house of their own and they would be where he felt they all belonged.

He gained his nursing qualifications and took up a nursing post at the local hospital. He loved his job even though it was hard work and he often had to work nightshifts, but he felt it was worth it. He couldn't spend as much time as he would have liked with his family, but it was for them, that he was working so hard. He was determined to give James and Abigail a better life than he had had, and he was succeeding.

The family moved into a three bedroomed council house on a new development in Bristol. Life was good, John was earning reasonable money and the children were growing up nicely. Julie started work as a teaching assistant and they were able to buy a car and even have a holiday now and then. They both worked hard and seemed happy enough, although perhaps they didn't see as much of one another as they would have liked.

It was about four years later that everything changed. John came home early from a shift one afternoon because he wasn't feeling too well, and found his best friend, Tom, in his bed with Julie. He completely lost it, dragged Tom out and threw him down the stairs, followed by his shoes and clothes. Tom staggered away, leaving Julie and John in the ruins of their marriage.

Julie tried to explain that she had felt for years that John no longer loved her. He was never there, always working. Tom had been there, and they had fallen in love. First of all, John couldn't believe what he was hearing. How could Julie think that he didn't love her? Everything he had been doing for years was so that he could take care of her and the children. He loved them all more than anything in the world, more than his own life. An anger bubbled up inside him that would never go away. He thought about the struggles he'd had to get to where he was today; the rejection by his own mother, the failures at school, losing his way and ending up addicted to drugs and then imprisoned, how he had struggled on his release to get back on his feet, with Alison's help, and then meeting Julie, his Julie, who had encouraged and supported him as he gained his qualifications. Now she had betrayed him, and it had all been for nothing.

He couldn't look at her. He had to get out of the house, or he feared he might hurt her. He ran for miles round the Bristol streets, down as far as the docks. He stood by the river, feeling that he might as well jump in and end it all. What was the point, he could never go through all that effort again. He was lost once more, just as he had been when his father had screamed out his rejection. He was a ten-year-old boy again and feeling just as impotent and hopeless. Of course, he knew he would have to carry on. He had the children to think about. Whatever had happened he was still their dad and they needed him.

Things however, went from bad to worse. He realised he would have to move out of the family home. He just couldn't share it with Julie. He couldn't look at her or even speak to her, it hurt him too much to even try and so he closed himself off from her and even from the children, who of course didn't understand what was going on. The next week he asked his mother if he could stay with her for a while. She said he could, as long as it was only until he sorted out somewhere else to live. He packed his bag and left Julie and his children, which broke his heart and his spirit.

One day, about six months later Julie asked to meet him at the coffee shop round the corner. He wondered what she wanted to see him about. Was it too much to hope that she might be having second thoughts and wanted him back? When they were sitting down at the table with their coffees, he rather nervously asked her why she had asked to meet him. She hesitated for a moment or two, obviously unsure how to put it, then blurted out that she wanted a divorce, adding that she and Tom wanted to move in together permanently.

John couldn't speak. His guts were tied in knots and his throat was too tight to let the words out. He thought about refusing but he knew he could never trust her again after this, so what would be the point. He nodded and she handed him the name and address of her solicitor. She told him to use adultery as the cause of the breakdown as she had no intention of protesting her innocence. What was done was done and she was prepared to acknowledge the fault lay with her. With that, Julie walked out of the coffee shop leaving John stunned by what had just happened.

Walking back to his mother's place he was in a state of shock. So that was it, everything he had ever wanted and worked for lay in ruins and as he thought about it, he could trace all of this right back to the moment he was born, when his birth mother had rejected him, sentencing him to this life he had been forced to live. Who knows what kind of life would have awaited him if she hadn't decided he wasn't worth keeping? He realised she was probably a single mum and that it may have been a difficult prospect for her to bring him up alone, but that was her choice. He hadn't had a choice and she had no right to risk the way his life might turn out, just to give herself an easy life.

As the weeks and months passed, the divorce went through unchallenged. He saw the children once a week, but it broke his heart all over again each time he had to pick them up from the house that had once been his home. He managed to stay off drugs, although he was tempted, but he did start to drink more. One evening when he turned up for a night shift, his nursing manager noticed that he appeared to be drunk and sent him home. In fact, he had drunk a couple of glasses of wine, which had caused him to be slightly hypoglycaemic making him appear to be very drunk. When he explained, he was lucky that his manager believed him. However he did suggest that maybe John should consider taking a break from nursing until he had managed to sort his life out and he felt forced to resign. Fortunately, as it later turned out, it didn't go down on his record as an official dismissal.

He felt that life had kicked him in the teeth once more. He struggled on, trying to stay sober so that he could still see the children. He got a job with a cleaning firm. The money was terrible, but it meant he could still pay his mother some rent but, unfortunately, still afford to drink. Life was a constant battle, trying to deal with his health issues whilst still drinking, and holding on to his job.

Then, after a couple of years, Julie wrote to tell him that she and Tom were going to emigrate to Australia. What more could life throw at him, he wondered. Now he would lose his children completely. He had a rubbish job, no home, no family and now he wouldn't even be able to be a part time dad and may never see James and Abigail again. He would never afford to visit Australia, and they may never come back to England. He was utterly desolate. They left England four months later, and to try to deal with the pain, John continued to drink. He just about managed to keep his job but his mother, understanding that being addicted to drink only led in one direction, told him that he would have to find somewhere else to live.

So here he was now, in this shabby bedsit, barely existing. As the weeks and months went by his anger continued to focus on the person who had steered his whole life in this disastrous direction: his birth mother, who had even given him diabetes, as he saw it. He now felt that if he were ever to sort his life out, he needed to find her. He needed to know why she had given him up, and to make her understand the consequences of the decision she took all those years ago.

Chapter 3

CORSTON

Now determined to find his birth mother, John began to make enquiries. The Social Services people told him he needed to apply to see his adoption file. He completed the form and posted it off. Three weeks later, he got a letter asking him to attend a meeting when someone would be able to go through his file with him.

At the meeting, he discovered that he had been born in a mother and baby unit called Sandylands, in Wiltshire. His mother's name at the time was Joan Simons, but as the social worker pointed out, it was more than likely that she would have subsequently married. The file didn't contain any details beyond the date of the adoption itself. Apparently, his adoptive parents had several interviews before it was agreed that they could adopt him, at that time, he was called Peter Simons. John couldn't help pointing out rather wryly, that things hadn't turned out too well with his adoptive parents, and perhaps their interviewing techniques could have done with revising somewhat. Not taking him up on that, the social worker asked him what he intended to do with the information he had just been given.

John told her he intended to find his birth mother. He needed to know why she had given him up. Being a father himself, although he had now lost his children because of circumstances, he told her he could not imagine actually choosing to give them up to a stranger. She felt it her professional duty to point out to him that he ought to tread carefully. Maybe his mother had told no one in her family about him and may not now wish to see him. He must be prepared for that and handle the situation with some sensitivity. Sensitivity, John thought to himself. What about my sensitivity? Whoever considered that? However, he said nothing, just nodding at her intervention, thinking that she was after all, only doing her job.

Back home in his bedsit, he took out his mobile phone, and figuring out that Joan Simons would now have a different name, searched the Births, Deaths and Marriages on a family search site. Quite soon he found that a Joan Simons, had married Arthur Kent in the village of Corston, which he knew was just outside Bath, not ten miles away, in 1979! The odds were that this was his mother. Of course, he didn't know whether she was still alive, but he calculated that she would only be about sixty years old. He then searched the Electoral Roll which brought up an entry for Joan Kent and by paying a small fee he was able to get her current address and phone number. This must be his birth mother!

He was amazed how easy this had been, but now he had to decide what to do with the information. Should he write to her, or phone before going to see her, he wondered. If he wrote, he reasoned, maybe she would say 'no' and then he may never get the chance to meet her, unless he went in for stalking her, which didn't seem like a good idea. If he rung her, she could hang up, thinking he was a crank. No, he decided, the only way to be sure of seeing her and talking to her was to go to the address on the Electoral Roll. He checked to see whether there was an Arthur Kent at the same address and when he discovered there wasn't, checked the death records and found out that he had died some years previously. This made things more straightforward. In case she hadn't told her wider family about him, it would be easier if she was alone when he called.

He decided he would go to Corston on the fol-lowing Monday. He was very excited and not a little nervous. Would she be happy to see him? He had seen some of the family reunion programmes on the television and invariably, mothers who had given up their babies at birth were overjoyed when their off-spring found them. He imagined how it might be like that with his mother. Perhaps he would finally feel he belonged to someone. Monday couldn't come soon enough. He checked the times of the buses to Bath and decided he would plan to arrive just after lunch time and would need to catch the one o'clock bus from the bus station.

John rose early on Monday, taking a long hot bath before any of the other residents were up and about. He dressed in the only decent clothes he possessed, a pair of chinos and a River Island sweatshirt he'd picked up at the charity shop. He was feeling very nervous. This day might prove to be a turning point in his life. Maybe at last he would be able to feel just like everyone else, part of his own family, not just an outsider, an observer of other people's lives.

He made himself some toast and marmalade and a cup of tea. Even though he didn't feel much like eating, he knew that as a diabetic he had to eat as regularly as possible. After breakfast he checked his sugar level and found that he needed to inject some insulin. He had never quite come to terms with inject-ing, but he knew he would have to go on doing it for the rest of his life.

He was soon striding down the street towards town and the bus station where he would catch the bus to Bath. It was a pleasant enough journey through the Somerset countryside and before too long he realised that the next stop would be his. He rang the bell, took a deep breath, thought here goes, and stood up as the bus pulled into the bus stop.

He stepped down onto the pavement, then took out his mobile phone to check the map showing his mother's address. Within a couple of minutes, he had arrived at the address. It was a detached house which looked as though it had once been two cottages. The garden was well tended, with a colourful array of flowers and shrubs and divided in two by a paved path. Now he was here, standing outside the gate, he was rooted to the spot, unsure whether he could go ahead with it. What if she rejected him again? Could he cope with that? He instantly dismissed the thought. Surely that wasn't possible? He squared his shoulders, breathed deeply, opened the gate, and stepped up to the cottage door.

John pressed the doorbell. He heard the chimes ringing somewhere in the distance. After some moments, the door was opened by a smart, well dressed woman of about sixty.

'Hello,' she said, 'can I help you?'

'Errr,' John tried to speak, but somehow the words wouldn't come.

'Is there some problem,' the woman asked, 'do you need help?'

John had rehearsed this moment so often over the last few weeks, but when it came to it, he didn't know what on earth to say. Finally, he blurted out.

'I'm looking for Joan Kent, who used to be Joan Simons.'

Looking puzzled, the woman said,

'Yes, I am Joan Kent, but I'm sorry, do I know you?' she asked.

'I'm Peter, Peter Simons as was,' he replied.

At first, the woman looked puzzled, but after a few moments her expression changed to something akin to panic.

'What? Peter? Oh my god!' she exclaimed, then quickly glancing up and down the street, which wasn't lost on John, said quickly, 'Well, you'd better come in.'

John followed her down the hall and into a living room. He instantly recognised that this was an affluent home. There were beautifully framed original paintings hanging on the walls, and his feet sank into the expensive carpet. A mahogany display cabinet was full of silver items and china figurines. Given his own circumstances he couldn't help but be impressed with the luxury of the place. It spoke of years of stability that only inherited wealth or a lifetime of substantial monthly salary cheques could produce. They both stood awkwardly, looking at each other, wondering where this conversation was going to go next.

'I don't know what to say,' Joan said. 'I never expected that I would ever see you again. Why have you come? How did you find me? What do you want?'

John sensed this wasn't going well. This was not the reaction he'd expected at all. She was supposed to say that she'd always wondered where he was, was he happy, and so on. Instead, she seemed defensive and even perhaps a little afraid. He told her that he didn't mean her any harm, he just needed some answers that only she could give. He needed to know why she had given him up.

'Look,' said Joan, 'it was all a long time ago, in another life.'

Anger surged in John's chest at that statement.

'It wasn't another life; it still is my life!' he exclaimed rather more loudly than he had intended.

Joan looked startled.

'Yes, of course, I mean...' she said softly, 'look, I didn't have a choice.'

'Well, I certainly didn't, did I? I don't understand how you could give me up, not having any idea what kind of a life I might have.'

Joan staggered backwards as though he had physically struck her, then reached behind her for the arm of the chair and flopped down into it.

Standing over her, John was now spurred on by his anger and launched into describing just how awful his life had been, disclosing far more than he had meant to do, even including the bit about his criminal activities. Joan was obviously very distressed.

After he had finished, Joan didn't know what on earth to say to this stranger who was her son.

As she looked up at him, she could see that he had had a difficult life. It was written all over his face.

'Peter,' she began.

'John, my name's John. No one's ever called me Peter.'

'I'm sorry, I don't know what to say,' she finally managed. 'I was on my own, my parents were in Hong Kong and didn't know about you. I was in the middle of my university degree in Manchester and had no means of supporting you.'

This statement did nothing to assuage John's anger. So, she hadn't even told her parents, his grandparents, that he existed! And given his own struggles to get an education and his thwarted ambitions, it struck him as pretty ironic that she had given him up so that she could finish her own university degree.

'So basically then, I was just an inconvenience?' he snarled.

'Oh my God, do you think it was an easy thing for me to do? Well, it wasn't. It was one of the hardest things I've ever had to do.'

'But you didn't have to do it, did you?' he responded quickly. 'Other women choose a different path. Other women think about the child's future, not just their own. You could have had no idea what kind of future I was going to have. You just walked off into your own predictable, cosy life.'

Joan didn't like his tone and was becoming anxious about the direction this was going.

'Look,' she declared, 'I think it's time you left now.'

'Is it really that easy?' John snapped, 'Can you really turn your back on me again? I want you to acknowledge me as your son. Surely you feel something?'

'It's not that easy,' she said, with some force now; she was beginning to get angry. She hadn't invited him back into her life. She thought about her daughter, Sophie, and her own mother, neither of whom knew anything about Peter. Yes, she was ashamed that she had given him up. She had always felt ashamed, which is why she had never been able to tell anyone what she had done. She couldn't now let him back into her life because it would mean that everyone would have to know that she had been able to give up her own first-born son. It was intolerable of him to place her in this position without any warning, after forty years!

John was still standing; she hadn't even asked him to sit down. He seemed to be waiting for her to say something more, but she knew she was unable to tell him what he needed to hear. She stood up and said, in a strong, determined voice.

'This won't work, you have to go now, please.'

John's anger had turned to a cold indifference. What was the point. This woman was nothing to him, except the cause of all his misery. He turned to leave, then noticed the two pictures side by side on the wall. Graduation photographs of two young women. One was obviously Joan, but he asked her who the other one was.

'That's my daughter, Sophie,' Joan said after a moment's hesitation.

His indifference now morphed into something else. He had a sister; one she did keep and who had been given everything he should have had. An education good enough to take her to university, and no doubt everything else she ever wished for. He was left with an icy determination to get his own back on this family.

He said nothing and left without a backward glance.

As he walked away from the cottage, he was feeling numb. So that was it. He would have to come to terms with the fact that his mother had abandoned him so that she could get on with her own privileged life. Well, it was obvious that from her point of view it was probably the best thing she had ever done, in spite of her protestations to the contrary. Her life had been a good one. Her academic aspirations were fulfilled, she had definitely chosen a good provider for a husband, her home demonstrated that fact, and as well as that, she had been given a second chance at motherhood. What more could she have wished for? Certainly not the inconvenience of a bastard child! No wonder she had rejected him. What possible use could he be to her? He was simply an embarrassment.

He decided to walk part of the way to Bristol to give himself time to think. As he walked, with each step the anger grew once more. Along with the anger, something else was evolving in his brain. How dare she reject him once again? She was obviously capable of loving her daughter, but not him. Well, in that case, his birth mother was now dead to him. In fact, the woman he had just met had killed her just as she had extinguished any hope he had fostered of feeling loved and wanted once more by her. With a kind of twisted logic, he felt that she should be punished for such an act. Somehow, somewhere he decided, he would find a way to exact justice for what she had just done.

After he had been to Corston, John could think of little else. He was unable to understand how any mother could reject her child. He knew what it was to lose his children through no fault of his own, but he was certain he could never have chosen to abandon them. He felt constantly angry but there was nowhere for his anger to go. He knew he couldn't approach her again. He wanted to punish her for the life she had sentenced him to, but he had no idea how he could do that if he wasn't in contact with her, and so, the anger festered within him.

Chapter 4

REGRETS

As John slammed the door behind him, Joan hurried into the hall and dropped the catch on the door. She went back into the sitting room and poured herself a whiskey. She never drank during the day, but decided she certainly needed one now.

She had been completely floored by Peter's appearance. Her emotions were all over the place. Many times over the years she had imagined what it might be like to come face to face with her little boy, but had never expected it, and certainly not like this. He had given her no warning. It was too much to expect her to welcome him with open arms. Surely, he must realise that she had had a life too, one that hadn't included him and involving other people whose feelings had to be considered as well?

Realising she now had no way of contacting him, even if she wanted to, she began to regret telling him to leave so abruptly. She began to think about all the questions she should have been asking him but hadn't. He had mentioned his own children, now in Australia because his wife had cheated on him. No wonder he was angry, and he obviously was. He must now be convinced that she hadn't given tuppence about him, either as a baby, or now. She felt ashamed all over again. He had reached out to her in his moment of greatest need and she had failed him once more.

Now she knew she could never, ever tell Sophie or her own mother about him. She thought about the shoe box in the attic. Over the years she had taken it out a few times, mostly since Arthur had died. She wouldn't have risked it while he was still around because she had never even plucked up the courage to tell him about Peter. What a coward I am, she thought. She determined to retrieve the box from the attic as soon as possible and, God forgive her, to destroy it. Breaking down in tears it was a good ten minutes before she calmed herself down.

The pain in her stomach suddenly struck. This was happening more often these days, she thought, particularly after a glass of something, putting it down to the whiskey. She knew she ought to get it checked out but hated doctors and hated hospitals even more, and so she had kept putting it off. Deciding to take something for it she stood up, then noticing herself in the mirror was startled by her appearance. Her face was red from crying but it wasn't just that. She looked older and thinner. She hadn't been eating too well which accounted for her weight loss. Probably just getting older, she thought sadly.

After taking a dose of antacid medicine she made herself a cup of tea and sat down on the window seat in the lounge to drink it. She glanced up at Sophie's graduation photo on the wall. Peter had stopped to look at it as he was leaving, asking who it was. One more painful realisation for him, she thought. The cruel irony was that Sophie would have been a wonderful sister for him. Joan knew that she had always wanted a brother or sister, and when she was younger, had frequently said so. Of course, because of complications when Sophie was born, Joan was unable to have further children, which she had always secretly thought of as some kind of punishment for giving Peter away. Just one more reason why she had never told Sophie about him. What a mess! Of course, the one who had suffered most, it turned out, was Peter, and now she had thrown away any chance to make amends to him.

She did consider, in spite of what she had said to him, whether to try to find out where he was living so that perhaps, over time, they could get to know one another. However, she instantly dismissed the thought because as she told herself, nothing had changed. She still couldn't contemplate telling either Sophie or her own mother that she had kept him secret for all these years. She must accept it and was trapped in this guilt for the rest of her life. This was the price she must pay for what she had done forty years ago. There would never be an end to it.

As for Peter, or John as he was now called, she prayed, and she wasn't given to praying very often, that he would find it in his heart to forgive her so that he could find some relief from the anger that was obviously eating away at him.

She was surprised to hear the clock in the hall strike four. It had been quite an afternoon. She did think about going up into the loft to get the shoebox, but decided she was feeling quite drained and not really up to clambering up and down the loft ladder today. She determined to do it tomorrow, or, if Sophie decided to come over as she often did on Tuesdays, she would definitely do it on Wednesday.

She must go and visit her mother soon, too. She was deteriorating rapidly now, and sometimes when Joan visited, she didn't seem to know her at first. She would tell her who she was of course, and her mother would nod vacantly. They would sit together for an hour or so, holding hands. Sometimes Joan would trim her nails and paint them for her. She seemed to like that, or at least, she seemed to enjoy the personal attention. Her mother's world was shrinking and soon it wouldn't even include her. It was always depressing for Joan, who could never escape the thought that one day, she might be in a similar situation, but she did love her mother and made a point of visiting her at least once a week.

She decided to go that evening. Somehow, she needed to be near her mother right now, even though she wouldn't find much comfort there. Lingering memories of the love she had always had from her mother would, she felt, soothe her troubled soul tonight.

So it turned out. That night her mother did seem to know her and as she took Joan's hand, started to stroke it, which she had never done before. Maybe somewhere in the twilight zone of her brain, there remained enough maternal instinct to cause her to want to reach out to comfort her daughter. Joan was comforted, and glad that she had come. She wondered; would it be safe for me to tell her about Peter? She wanted to do that more than anything before it was too late. In the end she decided that sadly, she couldn't risk it. She couldn't take the chance of her saying something to Sophie about it, nor could she risk her mother being upset inside without being able to express it, and so the secret remained.

Chapter 5

SOPHIE

The day began like any normal weekday. Sophie had woken up to find Charles' arms around her as usual and had nuzzled closer to him for a few minutes until the alarm clock insisted it was time to get up. She kissed him gently on the cheek and eased herself out from his embrace. He opened his eyes and smiled at her as she slipped on her dressing gown.

'Good morning you,' he said fondly.

'Hi there, shouldn't you be getting up too?' she asked. 'You said you wanted to go in to school early today, didn't you?'

'I do,' he replied, 'we've got the Ofsted crowd in.'

'Lucky you,' Sophie quipped as she walked through into the bathroom.

She showered and dressed quickly, then went upstairs to rouse the children. They slept in the two bedrooms on the second floor of their Georgian town house. As she climbed the stairs she glanced out of the window on the landing, as she invariably did. The view was exquisite and always moved her. Indeed, the view had been one of the reasons they had chosen this particular house when Charles was appointed head of St Mark's primary school. It meant a considerable increase in his salary and they had felt it was finally time to fulfil their dream of buying one of the beautiful Georgian properties for which the city was famous. She was proud and happy that she and Charles had come so far and achieved so much. They would be able to give Isabella and Henry a good life, here in this lovely city of Bath.

The house they had chosen was halfway up one of the seven hills that held the city. It was over 200 years old and was built from beautiful Bath stone mined from the very hill it stood upon. There was a huge family room in the basement, underground at the front, but at the back, opening onto a garden leading down to the Kennet and Avon canal. Beyond that, there was a wonderful view out over the city. The four storeys provided ample room for a growing family, where everyone could enjoy their own space. She had to admit there were downsides though. For one thing it was a long way from the basement to the children's rooms. Far too easy for them to ignore her when she called them down for dinner, and quite a climb to find them, whenever they did.

This was a small price to pay though, for the endless pleasure of living in such a beautifully proportioned, elegant house. Whenever she had a few minutes to spare she would sit on the first floor in what in earlier times would have been the drawing room, simply enjoying being there and gazing out over the city with its many church steeples, Georgian terraces, and the Royal Crescent and the Abbey in the distance. Life was good and Sophie was happy here.

Today, she thought, as she prepared the children's packed lunches, she would visit her mum, as she often did on Tuesdays. She lived in Corston, a village just off the Bristol road. She hadn't been too well lately with some kind of digestive problem, as yet undiagnosed. She would try to persuade her to visit her doctor.

'Come on, you two!' she shouted up the stairs, 'Breakfast's ready!'

It wasn't, quite, but she always allowed at least ten minutes for them to clatter down the stairs after she had shouted them. She popped their eggs into the boiling water and buttered some bread, cutting it into soldiers, just as they liked. Today she popped two more eggs in as well. Charles would need something inside him if he were to face Ofsted, she mused. She called them all once more and was pleased to hear them trotting down the stairs, always jumping the last two steps on every flight, for the sheer joy of doing so.

'Not sure I've got time love,' Charles told her.

'Come on, it won't take you a minute, you'll work better with something inside you.' she replied.

She glanced at her children as she ate her egg. Isabella and Henry were her pride and joy. They would be nine this year. There had been no twins in either family, and when she found she was pregnant it just never occurred to her that there might be two babies growing inside her. It was at the first scan that they were told the news and it was a shock, but a nice one. They had always intended to have two children and now they would have them both at the same time. Isabella was fair haired, and Henry's hair was dark, like Charles's. She was always amazed that twins could be so different and not just in colouring, but also temperamentally. Henry had boundless energy and was always looking for the next adventure, whereas Isabella would far rather have her nose stuck in a book.

Charles finished his egg in record time, gave her a peck on the cheek and picking up his briefcase from the study next to the front door, set off for work. The children were sent to clean their teeth in the downstairs cloakroom before putting on their coats and shoes. Sophie still liked to walk them to school even though they kept insisting that they didn't need taking anymore. The short journey took them down to the canal and along the towpath for fifty yards or so before dropping down steep steps, then under the railway arch to the busy main road. There was a lollipop man at the crossing, but Sophie knew how impulsive children could be.

She left them outside the school, telling them to enjoy their day and she would be there to meet them at the end of it. There were one or two familiar faces at the school gates, but as yet she hadn't been living here long enough to make any friends. She watched them walk through the gates, then waving to them one last time, made her way back to the road and up the hill to home. She cleared away the breakfast things and loaded the dishwasher, then went upstairs to tidy the beds before getting ready to visit her mum. She rang to let her know she was coming, and predictably, Joan, who loved to feed her at every opportunity, said she would make some soup for their lunch.

Half an hour later she was parking up outside Joan's house. It was an old cottage, one of the oldest in the village. Sophie had literally been born there and loved the old place. Warm memories enveloped her as soon as she walked through the front door. She had had a happy childhood, never wanting for anything. Her only regret was that she had no brothers or sisters. Her parents were kind and loving, but she missed having someone her own age to play with and with whom to share her secrets.

As soon as Sophie saw Joan, she realised something must be wrong. She looked pale and drawn.

'What's wrong Mum, you don't look too well,' she said, after they had hugged each other.

'Oh, I'm alright,' Joan told her, 'I've just been a bit off colour, that's all.'

'Well, you need to let the doctor take a look at you. Please Mum. Just to set my mind at rest. Shall I give the surgery a ring? I could go with you if they have a slot free today.'

Although not too keen, Joan could see Sophie was

worried about her and decided it would probably be best to get checked out.

'OK then, you can give them a call. The number's in the speed dial.'

The doctor's receptionist said Sophie her Mum could come in at one o'clock, so they had time to have their lunch first. Sophie noticed that her mother only ate a couple of spoons full of soup before declaring she had eaten enough. This wasn't like her, she thought, she'd always had a good appetite.

The doctor gave Joan a thorough examination and decided it would be a good idea to investigate further. He emailed the hospital in Bristol requesting certain tests and told Joan they would be sending her appointments soon.

As she drove back home, Sophie had to admit she was rather worried about her mum. She'd never really been ill before, apart from the odd bout of flu and an episode of shingles which, while painful, was not what Sophie would regard as serious. Funny to think of mum growing old, she reflected, but something she supposed she would have to get used to, and to prepare for.

She arrived back in Bath just in time to park up and walk to the school gates before Henry and Isabella came bounding out, all smiles and clutching their latest artwork, most likely to be placed on the fridge door for everyone to admire. Sophie smiled fondly at them and roundly praised their efforts.

A couple of weeks later, Sophie had taken her

mother for the tests and then to revisit the doctor, once the results were in. The news was not good. Apparently, they had identified a stomach ulcer which needed immediate surgery as it was in danger of rupturing, which could be very dangerous. Joan was horrified. She hated hospitals and had never actually had to stay in one. She'd given birth to Sophie at home and had never before had any major illnesses. Of course, she accepted that it had to be done and two weeks later she got the appointment for her operation at the hospital in Bristol. Sophie felt Joan hadn't seemed herself for a few weeks, putting it down to the fact that she was in some pain and was relieved that Joan's health problems would soon be dealt with.

Joan was not looking forward to her stay in hospital one little bit. She knew the operation had to be done. It was getting worse. She had been particularly stressed since Peter had appeared which she knew wasn't helping. She thought again about the shoebox which she still hadn't managed to deal with, just not feeling up to climbing into the loft. She determined to sort it out as soon as she was well enough.

Sophie picked her up on the day of her appointment and drove her to the hospital and although Joan seemed nervous as they arrived, Sophie reassured her she would be fine and she would be over to see her the next day, once the operation was over.

The surgery wasn't performed until later the next day as there had been some hold up in theatre. When Sophie rang later that evening to find out how it had gone, they told her that the operation had been successful, and her mother had recovered from the anaesthetic but was now sleeping peacefully. They suggested that perhaps it would be best if she visited the next day.

Chapter 6

PAYBACK

John had just come on to the night shift at the hospital and had been asked to deal with a spillage on ward 10, the female surgical ward. It was as he walked past one of the side wards that he saw her. She was the last person he expected to see here, in a hospital bed. She was apparently asleep. It was quite early in the evening, so it was unusual for patients to be asleep yet, unless they were recovering from surgery, which he assumed she was.

He dealt with the spillage in the main ward and then went back to the small room where he waited to be called out for any urgent cleaning job that came in. When he had seen her there, the anger that was never far from the surface bubbled up again. Since her rejection of him three weeks ago he couldn't put it out of his mind. It was like a cancer growing inside him. He wanted to make her pay. She had given him this life he'd been forced to live, and this unhealthy body that meant he had to 'stab' himself every day for the rest of it. He wondered how she would like it, then decided she would never have coped with what he'd had to contend with.

As he sat there, he thought about the abuse he'd suffered from his 'father', how he had drifted into drugs and crime ending up in prison. Even when he'd struggled so hard to get his life back on track, in the end his wife had betrayed him, and he'd lost his children. All this, the whole sequence of events he traced back to the moment that woman had handed him over to strangers. Even then, when he had reached out to her at the lowest point in his miserable life, she had once again rejected him.

Well, this was his chance. Payback time. He had his insulin with him, he never went anywhere without it. Ironic really, that this was how it was to be done.

He waited until about three o'clock in the morning when he knew from experience that unless there was an emergency the nurses would be chatting at their station in the main ward. If he were careful, he would be able to slip un-noticed into her room. In the event it was all too easy and within seconds he found himself beside her bed. Without hesitation, he pulled out the syringe he had prepared and administered her a substantial dose. She was soundly asleep and had only murmured slightly as he inserted the needle. He knew exactly what he was doing. From his nurse's training and his own use of the stuff, that unless she was also diabetic and in need of it, the amount he was giving her would be fatal. He also knew that it would leave no trace in her body for the pathologist to find at post-mortem, which would most certainly be carried out. It would be just another unexplained death in the hospital; a rare, but not unheard-of occurrence.

After he had finished, he didn't wait around to see her reaction to the injection but left swiftly and hurried back to the lift. He was certain no one had seen him. It was finished, and he felt a huge relief. Now she had truly gone. She was not only dead to him, but to the whole world, and he was glad. Maybe now he really could get on with his life.

As he walked home after his shift, for the first time, he thought about her daughter. He was sorry she had to be hurt, but at least, he thought, she would now know what it was like to have no mother.

At eight o'clock the next morning Sophie received a phone call to say that her mother had passed away during the night. Her legs buckled under her, the colour drained from her face and she dropped down into the dining chair. Charles asked her what was wrong, but she couldn't speak. After a few moments, she motioned to him to come out into the garden, out of earshot of the twins.

'It's mum,' she managed, 'Oh Charles, she's gone!'

'What do you mean, gone?' he asked quickly.

'They've just told me that she passed away in the night!'

'Oh, my God, Sophie. That's terrible. Did they say what happened?'

Sophie told him that they had given her no details but suggested she go up to the hospital straight away, if possible. She couldn't believe it. It didn't make any sense. Her mum had come through the operation without any complications. That's what they had told her. No way should her life have been in danger. Sophie thought about how she had told her mum everything would be fine. If she hadn't taken her to the doctor, this wouldn't have happened. Already she was blaming herself.

The children were more or less ready for school, having just finished breakfast and Charles quickly took charge of them, saying he would drop them at school so that Sophie could go straight over to Bristol to find out exactly what had happened.

An hour later she was sitting opposite the consultant who had performed the operation. He told her that as far as he was concerned everything had gone well. There had been no problems with the procedures he had carried out and when he had last seen Joan, she had come round from the anaesthetic and was settling down to a good night's sleep. At this point he said, he could offer no explanation as to what had happened, in which case he would have to recommend that an autopsy be carried out to determine the cause of her death.

Sophie was devastated. She needed answers but apparently as of now, there were none. She was upset that there would have to be an autopsy, horrified at what it would entail, but at the same time, she knew it would have to be done if they were ever to find out why her mother had died.

In the event, the autopsy, which was carried out the next day, revealed nothing. There seemed to be no discernible reason why Joan had died. The funeral was held the following week and Sophie was still in shock. She had been unable to cry. There was plenty of anger of course, and guilt that she had encouraged Joan to see the doctor in the first place. Charles was wonderful. He made all the arrangements for the funeral and let everyone who needed to, know what they were. The children were upset. Joan had been a big part of their lives and it was the first death they had experienced. Sophie kept them off school for a couple of days but then decided they would be better off being occupied in school. She and Charles decided they ought to be at the funeral to help them process their grief and at the crematorium they sat, one each side of Sophie, and cried together for what they would never do again with their grandma.

There was an inquest of course, but without any evidence, it was recorded as a death from unknown causes. Sophie was just not satisfied with this outcome. There had to be some reason why she had lost her mum. Someone had to be responsible and she would never be satisfied until she knew who, even if it had been a genuine error. She would not be able to come to terms with it until she had a full explanation of what had happened. She and Charles demanded to meet a senior manager to ask them to hold a full enquiry about Joan's treatment and care.

It was some weeks later that they were ushered into a large room with a table in the centre. Round the table were several medical looking people and a couple of executive types. The woman at the head of the table introduced herself as Gloria Harper, the Chief Executive of the Trust. She introduced each of the people sitting round the table and then offered her deepest sympathy for Sophie's loss, which seemed genuinely meant. She went on to explain that they had carried out a thorough investigation into her mother's death. They had interviewed all the staff who had been involved at every level of her care. They had reviewed all the records of her medication and treatments and had spoken at length to her surgeon, who was in fact, sitting opposite Sophie. However, she said, they had been unable to find anything untoward and still could not offer any explanation as to why Joan had died. Ms Harper said that they were there today to hand them the report, to answer any further questions Sophie or Charles might have, and to assure them that everything possible had been done to give them the answers they needed.

Sophie asked whether anyone had been with her mother when she died. The Sister sitting next to the surgeon looked a little uncomfortable and explained that in fact her mother had passed away in the night between routine checks on her at 3am and 6am. Sophie was horrified.

'You mean after she had had surgery during the day, she had been left alone for three hours without anyone checking on her? Surely that can't be normal, can it?'

The Sister looked at the Surgeon and he replied.

'Well, in your mother's case, the surgery had gone well, and she had recovered from the anaesthetic. She was sleeping peacefully, and all her vital signs were good. In such a case she would not have been put on constant observation and checking her every three hours during the night would have been perfectly normal. There was really nothing to indicate that she would need closer observation.'

'But obviously something must have been wrong. What actually happened to cause her death? You must have some idea. Did her heart just stop beating and if so, why?' Charles asked him.

'Well, her heart did certainly stop beating, but I'm afraid we have been able to find no answer as to why. I'm so sorry that I can't be more helpful. Sometimes these things just happen. It is rare, but it does happen.'

Both Sophie and Charles realised there was nothing more to be done here and they would just have to accept it. They picked up the report, thanked the CEO and the rest of the assembled company and took their leave.

Sophie now knew this was something she would have to come to terms with, but that may take some time. Of course, she still occasionally wondered what had actually happened during that night, and whether Joan would have known anything about it. It gave her some comfort to tell herself that probably she just passed away peacefully in her sleep, but it wasn't always possible for her to believe that.

Realising she had taken matters at the hospital as far as she could, Sophie decided the time had come to start to sort out Joan's affairs. There was the cottage to think about. She hadn't been back there since the day she had taken her mother to the hospital. Charles dealt with the death certificate and sorted out the insurance policies. Joan had always made sure they were kept in a safe place and had told Sophie exactly where they were, and so it turned out.

Now it was time to think about what to do with the cottage and all Joan's effects. She was dreading going there. How could she enter that place that had always been warm and full of love for her, and find it cold and empty? It would have to be sold, of course, but first it had to be cleared and that meant delving into all of her mother's possessions. Every cupboard and drawer would have to be sorted through, and the thing she was dreading most, the loft, would have to be cleared. She knew that her parents had stored many things in the loft. It would be a record of their lives together. Her schoolbooks, family holiday photographs, photographs of people who had gone, some of whom she had known and some who died long before she was born. It was going to be quite a job. The alternative would be to pay someone to clear everything out of the house, but she couldn't do that. Her mother's things deserved more respect than to be simply thrown into a skip. No, it was the last duty she could perform for her mum and she would do it with love.

Between looking after the family and the house, it took Sophie several weeks to sort through the cupboards and drawers at Joan's cottage, making decisions about what was going to charity, what she would keep and what would just have to go. Finally, all that remained was the loft. One Sunday she left Charles looking after the children and decided to tackle it. There was a pull-down ladder that her father had installed, which made for easy access. Thankfully, he had also rigged up some lighting. The sight greeting her as she reached the trapdoor was daunting. There were numerous piles of cardboard boxes, an old trunk, boxes of toys that she had long forgotten, including her favourite doll they had bought her for her fifth birthday, which was sitting rather forlornly on top of one of the boxes. There were two or three old brown suitcases, an ancient record player and a red rug she remembered being in front of the fire years ago.

As she climbed into the loft, the familiar musty smell of old books, and woodsmoke that had seeped through the chimney stack over the years, assaulted her senses. It prompted memories of forays into the loft with her dad when, as a special treat, he had allowed her to help him search for some precious treasure or other. Thoughts of her dad brought recollections of past Christmases and birthdays flooding back, and she allowed herself to remember her parents' love which had surrounded her all her life, and how that love was now gone forever. Not for the first time, Sophie broke down in tears. After some time, she calmed down and sitting on one of the suitcases, wondered where on earth she could begin.

Chapter 7

REVELATION

She realised she would need Charles to help her to remove the things from the loft as it would all need to be carried down the ladder somehow. However, she felt she could be usefully employed sorting through it all, placing things to keep and things to discard in separate piles. It actually turned out to be easier than she had expected. Most of the boxes contained books and a few of them, old photographs. These could all be taken straight to their own house to be sorted later. She opened the old tin trunk and found that it was full of household linen. Lifting them out one by one to see if any of them were still usable, she found a couple of bedspreads, some sheets and pillowcases, a woollen blanket and a couple of pillows.

Her curiosity was aroused as, right at the bottom under a tartan car rug, she found a taped-up cardboard shoe box. It looked out of place underneath all the linen, and she quickly lifted it out to see what was in it. She did feel it was a bit of an intrusion to break the tape. Her mother had obviously not intended it to be opened, but she was even more curious when she saw the contents. There were several items of baby clothes, a pair of tiny bootees, and a knitted cardigan. Right in the bottom of the box was a photograph of a baby, obviously new-born. At first, she thought it must be of her, until she turned the photograph over to see if it explained who the baby was. Written on the back was Peter, 8pm, 26th May 1972, Sandylands.

Who was this child? Of course, the most obvious conclusion would be that her mother had given birth to him. Then she realised that the date in 1972 was five years before her mother and father were married. Perhaps her mother had had an illegitimate child. But what had happened to him? Her head was spinning with possibilities. Maybe he had died, or maybe her mum had given him up for adoption? Perhaps he wasn't hers after all. Then it occurred to her that if he had been adopted, maybe she could find him. She remembered how lonely she had sometimes been growing up and how she had longed for a brother or a sister. The chance that she may have a brother somewhere excited her and she knew she would have to search for him. Probably Sandylands was a nursing home where he was born, and his name then would have been Peter Simons as he would probably have been given her mother's maiden name at birth. It should be fairly easy to pick up his trail, as she had his name and date and place of birth.

She replaced the items in the trunk and carefully repacking the shoe box, decided she'd done enough sorting for today. In any case she could do no more until Charles was with her, so she tidied up the bits and pieces lying around, and taking the shoe box, climbed carefully down the ladder. She was eager to tell Charles about this amazing discovery and her plan to look for someone who may turn out to be the big brother she had always wanted.

When Sophie arrived home, the children were playing up in their rooms, which gave her the chance to show Charles what she had found. In the event, his reaction wasn't quite what she had expected. He immediately took up a negative position, telling her it was all a long time ago and maybe things were best left as they were. It was her mother's secret and if she had wanted her to know, she would have told her all about it. Sophie, however, was in no doubt that she must find this person, whatever it took. She was convinced her mother would have wanted that. To give up a baby is a traumatic thing to do and she was certain that if her mother were alive now, and she offered to help her to find him, she would not have hesitated for a moment. She would do it for her mother. Once this thought had settled into her brain there was no going back. This was a mission she had to complete for her mother's sake. Knowing his wife as he did, Charles soon realised it was useless to try to reason her out of it and that he may as well support her in her quest.

The weeks since her mother's death had been hard for Sophie. She was still angry about the lack of any answers as to why she had died, and at the same time, she was consumed with guilt because she had instigated the train of events that had led to her death. She missed her mother terribly. She had been her chief confidant, having no sisters to share her fears and hopes with. Somehow the discovery of the box and the quest she was determined to embark upon seemed in some strange way to give her a chance to turn the tragedy of her mother's death into something meaningful. If she could find her brother, as she now definitely thought of him, she would be doing something for her mother that she would now never be able to do for herself. This gave her some comfort and sense of purpose that distracted her from the grief and made it easier to bear.

The very next day Sophie started to plan her search. She would begin by locating 'Sandylands.' She reasoned it wouldn't be too far away. Her mother had been brought up in Bristol and would probably have been living there when the baby was born. Then the thought struck her that of course, she would have been twenty years old, and actually at Manchester University at the time. If the baby was born in May, it was possible that he may have been born in Manchester or somewhere nearby. Sophie wondered whether

her grandparents would actually have known about the child. She remembered that her grandfather was in the Diplomatic Corps and often worked overseas. It's possible that they may have been out of the country when she gave birth to Peter. Maybe that explains the fact that his existence had been kept a secret from everyone. Sophie knew that in the seventies there were many mother and baby nursing homes where unmarried mothers could go to give birth, and often give their babies up for adoption immediately, without ever bringing them home. Maybe Sandylands was such a place.

Once she had dropped the children off at school, Sophie went straight home and turned on the computer in the study. She made herself a cup of tea and settled down to some desk research, trying to locate Sandylands. First of all, she pulled up a list of nursing homes anywhere in the country, which revealed nothing. Then she wondered if Sandylands now had another function. Maybe it had become a care home for the elderly, or even been turned into a private home. She searched the name 'Sandylands', which brought up a host of results, mainly for a holiday resort company, but there were also four more promising ones. There was a care home in London and another one in Scotland which seemed to be a private home. The third one was a boutique hotel in Wiltshire and the fourth was in Bolton in Lancashire and appeared to be a retirement home for the elderly. She felt the most promising were the properties in Wiltshire, not being too far from Bristol, and Bolton, being close to Manchester.

The next step, she reasoned, would be to give them a call to find out if either of them had ever been a mother and baby home. So, what if one of them had, she wondered. What did she hope to find out from the current owners? It wasn't likely they would have any records from forty years ago, and even if they did have some books tucked away somewhere, would they be prepared to dig them out and search through them for her? Not very likely, she thought.

Maybe there was another way. She was quite interested in ancestry research and had done a bit of delving into her father's family history. She wondered if she might be able to find a birth record in the Births, Marriages and Deaths database. Peter would probably have been registered as Peter Simons, using her mother's maiden name. She checked the database and to her delight there was an entry for Peter Simons, in the April to May listing for 1972, giving his mother's maiden name as Simons! Her heart skipped a beat as she saw that the district where he was born was Wiltshire. Surely the boutique hotel in Wiltshire must now be favourite for Peter's place of birth. This was excellent news. She could easily book into the hotel for a night or two, if Charles would look after the twins, when she would be able to have a face-to-face conversation with the hotel owners, who might then be willing to help her. Even if they had no records, they may be able to give her details of previous owners. Still, it might be useful before visiting the place, to find out whether it had actually ever been a mother and baby home.

She gave the number a ring and spoke to the receptionist who had picked up the phone. Explaining that she had a rather strange request and was trying to find out whether the hotel had ever been a nursing home, or a mother and baby home during the seventies. The receptionist was helpful enough but not aware what the place had been so long ago. However, she said she would put her through to the hotel owner, Mr Bradshaw, as he may be able to help her. He did indeed prove to be more helpful and told Sophie that he believed it had been some kind of a nursing home at one time. Sophie explained she was trying to find information about a baby who she believed had been born there. He thought there might be some old records in the attic and offered to pop up there to have a look and would ring her back. She gave him her number and hung up. She made herself another cup of tea and a sandwich and within half an hour, Mr Bradshaw called back. He told her that there were quite a few old accounts books and the like, in boxes in the attic. She asked if he might allow her to look through them if she booked in with them for a night. He said that he would be only too pleased. Sophie told him she would sort out a date when it would be convenient to visit the hotel and would get back to him shortly.

Pleased with the progress so far, Sophie determined to discuss it with Charles when he came home and if he were agreeable, she could take her trip to Wiltshire over the coming weekend. She would book in for one night as she would need to be back home by Sunday evening. However, if she left early on Saturday, she would have the best part of two days to delve into the records, which should be plenty of time to find the information if indeed there was any.

When Charles arrived home that evening, he was not one bit surprised to hear that Sophie had already begun her search and had come up with a likely venue for the baby's birth. Of course, he told her, he would be fine looking after the twins. In fact, he may take them to stay at his parent's place overnight. They lived down on the coast in Dorset and the children loved going there whenever they got the chance. The beach at Weymouth was their favourite playground and Grannie and Grandad spoiled them unashamedly. He might even take them down on the train, as an extra treat.

So that was settled. Sophie immediately rang Sandylands and booked herself in for Saturday night, explaining that she would be arriving by lunchtime in order to start looking through the old records, as Mr Bradshaw had agreed she could. The receptionist said that was fine and they would try to have her room ready by midday.

The children were excited when Charles told them

he was taking them down to Grannie and Grandad's at the weekend, particularly when they realised, they were going by train. Of course, they wanted to know why Sophie wasn't going too, but accepted the explanation that she had work to do.

Sophie spent the next day at the cottage, taking bags to the charity shop and loading the car with any bits and pieces she wanted to keep. The attic would have to wait until the weekend after next, when Charles had promised to help her to get everything down. She would have to book the house clearance people to take away anything that was left, and the cottage could be put up for sale. As things stood, she was the next of kin and whatever money there was, would come to her. Of course, the thought occurred to her as she was locking the front door, that if she did find her half-brother, he might be entitled to a share of the estate, although she understood that this may not be the case if he had been legally adopted.

It felt strange for her to be considering such things, but then the whole situation felt weird. With the discovery she may have a brother, her self-concept had shifted. It was really quite disorientating. She had always been an only child with no need to think about anyone else. Even though of course, both her parents were now dead, the family unit still formed the framework for her identity. Her place in the triangular family had felt secure. Now the shape of the family and her place in it had changed. There may soon be another person sharing that space. For the first time, she felt a little apprehensive, realising that finding him may well change her life.

She did not realise just how true that was to become.

Chapter 8

SANDYLANDS

Saturday dawned bright and warm. Sophie had woken early, anxious to get Charles and the children off on their trip so that she could concentrate on her own expedition to Wiltshire. She woke the children, laying out the clothes they would need for the day and packing their pyjamas, swim things and change of clothes, in their rucksacks. They were excited and didn't need telling twice to get washed and dressed and then hurry down to breakfast.

Down in the kitchen she made herself a mug of tea. Opening the patio doors, she strolled out to the end of the garden and stood, surveying the city below. It was a warm, bright July morning with a slight heat haze hanging about in the valley below. It was going to be a lovely day for Charles and the children at the coast and she half wished she were going with them. However, she soon dismissed the thought and, sipping her tea began to wonder what her own day would bring. By the time she came home tomorrow would she be any nearer to finding Peter?

She was woken from her reverie by the children bounding out into the garden demanding breakfast as they didn't want to miss their train. She turned, smiled indulgently at them, and strode back to the kitchen to prepare their cereal and toast. Charles was already putting the kettle back on. She kissed him affectionately on the cheek and said,

'It's going to be a lovely day, but it looks as though it could be a hot one. Make sure you put plenty of sun cream on the children.'

'Understood, Ma'am,' he said with a smile, giving a mock salute.

While she prepared breakfast, they chatted about the arrangements for the day.

'What time did you say your train was?' she asked.

'Oh, not until ten thirty, but I will need to buy the tickets, so we need to be at the station for ten fifteen at the latest,' he replied.

'I can drop you there on my way out then. I was intending to get away around ten myself.'

'That's great,' Charles said, 'and we hope to get the four fifteen from Weymouth tomorrow which is due back in Bath about half six, but I'll give you a ring to confirm that once we're underway. Do you think you'll be back in time to pick us up? If not, we can always get a taxi.'

'Good heavens, yes of course I'll be back. It shouldn't

take me too long to find what I'm looking for so I'm expecting to be home by lunchtime tomorrow, at the latest,' Sophie assured him.

She called to the children, who were playing around in the garden,

'Come on you two! Breakfast's ready!'

They ran towards the doors, trying to beat each other through the gap. Henry got there first as usual. Everything turns into a game with them, thought Sophie, realising that this was partly what she'd missed out on, not having a brother or sister around. Funny, but until recently, she hadn't really given voice to such thoughts. Now, they kept springing out at her at the oddest of times.

The children got stuck into their breakfasts with gusto. Sophie wished they would show half as much enthusiasm on a school morning. She had to be be-hind them every minute then to keep them focussed. Now, with the prospect of a train journey followed by the seaside and Grannie and Grandad, they needed no such encouragement and were soon shouting,

'Finished! Can we go now?!'

'Go and clean your teeth then pack your brushes and toothpaste in the toilet bag in the cloakroom and put it into your rucksack Henry,' Sophie instructed.

'OK mum!' he threw back over his shoulder as he ran to the cloakroom, hoping to beat his sister to the tap. A bit of a scuffle ensued, but eventually they came to an arrangement to share the sink and got on with it.

'Don't build your hopes up too high love,' Charles said to Sophie as they ate their toast, 'you know it's a long shot, don't you? If he was adopted, it's not easy to get hold of the details. They're very cagey about disclosing anything to the birth family, or so I believe.'

'Yes, I know. I've watched enough family tracing programmes to know this will only be the first step, but it's all I've got at the moment. Don't worry about me, I'll be fine,' she reassured him, 'I know this is likely to be a long road, and in any case may not end up the way I would like it to.'

She checked the children's rucksacks to make sure they had everything, and that Henry had put the toilet bag in as well. They had also packed a holdall they always liked to take to the seaside, with buckets and spades and little moulds to create stars and shell shapes to decorate their sandcastles. Isabella had also packed a book to read on the train and Henry had a couple of puzzle books to keep him occupied.

Charles went upstairs to bring his own bag down while Sophie cleared away the breakfast things and loaded the dishwasher, then went upstairs to brush her hair, apply her makeup and to collect her own bag that she had packed the night before.

Fifteen minutes later she pulled up in the carpark of the railway station. Getting out, she opened the back doors for the children to climb out. She ensured that they had everything, then gave them both a hug, telling them to have a lovely time and be sure to tell her all about it when they got back. Charles bent down and gave her a kiss, wishing her luck. She told him to give her love to his mum and dad and kissed his cheek, then off they went.

She took a moment to watch them disappear into the station, giving them one last wave as they did so. Taking a deep breath and resetting her mind to the task ahead, she worked out that the best route to take would be up the Bathwick Hill Road out of town, turning left at the roundabout, down Brassknocker Hill and out towards Warminster. In any case, she now set the satnav to the postcode of Sandylands, which told her the journey would take her about an hour and fifteen minutes, traffic permitting. Finally, she set off towards what she felt might be a slightly uncertain future, but one she knew she must pursue.

As it happened, the roads were pretty clear, even the infamous A303 which she picked up about half-way there. She saw that thankfully most of the traffic was heading the other way, probably making for the coast on such a beautiful summer day. It was about eleven forty-five when she reached the turnoff towards Sandylands. Realising she was a little early, she stopped at an inviting looking pub to get something to eat. It turned out to be a good choice. It was an old country pub which had a welcoming air as they so often do. There was an interesting menu of light lunches and she ordered a ham and cheese toasted sandwich with a Greek salad, and a pot of tea. By the time she had finished and settled the bill it was almost one o'clock. After freshening up in the washroom, she was on her way again.

She pulled up outside Sandylands at about one twenty. Perfect timing, she thought. It had obviously once been a private home, but that would have been a couple of hundred years ago. It had the familiar Georgian proportions she was very used to and standing in its own grounds was approached along a short drive. The garden was more like a small country estate, with lawns, a small lake, and woodlands. Very pleasant, Sophie thought to herself.

Then it occurred to her that her mother may well have stood outside this building forty years earlier. What state of mind was she in, Sophie wondered. She was probably afraid, about to give birth to a baby who she would have to give up to strangers after carrying him inside her for months. She may have wondered if she would be able to do it when the time came. Sophie was certain that she personally could not, but then, she reminded herself, times were different then. Life wasn't easy for single mums, and without IVF there were lots of people unable to have children and desperate to adopt new-borns.

Taking her holdall out of the boot Sophie entered the hotel and walked up to the reception desk where a well-groomed young woman was looking at her expectantly. She explained who she was and that she was booked in for the one night. The receptionist checked the computer in front of her and told her that her room was ready, and she was in Room 21, then handed her the room key. She asked whether she would be eating dinner in the hotel, and would she be wanting breakfast in the morning. Sophie said yes, on both counts.

Sophie picked up her bag to go up to her room but before heading for the stairs, asked the receptionist whether the manager, Mr Bradshaw, was around. The young woman said he had just left but had said he would be back in an hour or so. Sophie explained that she needed to speak with him when he returned, and would she let him know that she had arrived. The girl agreed to do so, and to let Sophie know when he was in the building.

Climbing the stairs to the first floor, Sophie located room 21 which turned out to be a pleasant if smallish room to the side of the hotel, with a tall window looking out across the gardens to the woodlands beyond. The sun was streaming in and Sophie sat down in a chair by the window to enjoy the view and to relax a little. She took out her mobile phone and called Charles. He answered quickly, asking whether she had arrived at the hotel. From the background noise she could tell they were at his parent's place. She could hear his mother calling the children to come and eat their lunch. She smiled to herself. Feeding them all would have been top of Mary's agenda. It always was. She loved looking after people, particularly her only son and his grandchildren.

Sophie told him about the journey and what

Sandylands was like, then asked him how the train journey had been. He told her that it was definitely the best way to travel with two lively children. He had even been able to read his newspaper! She told him she was hoping to speak to Mr Bradshaw when he returned to the hotel and then hopefully, would be able to get stuck into searching through the stuff in the attic. Charles said they would all be going down to the beach after lunch and he would ring her later to find out how she was getting on. With that, they said their goodbyes and hung up.

Sophie freshened up so that she would be ready to go and meet Mr Bradshaw as soon as he was able to see her. Sitting down by the window again she took out her phone to do a bit of research on tracing people who had been adopted. She loved watching the family tracing programmes on the television and knowing it would be impossible for her to access Peter's adoption files herself, understood she would need to use some kind of intermediary. Entering the search term 'how to trace an adopted child' she discovered that there was a Government register where she could search for Peter in case he had subscribed to it in an attempt to find his birth mother. In addition, there were many agencies who could act as an intermediary to search for him if that route proved to be a dead end. So, it looked like there were many options, once Sophie had satisfied herself that Joan had given birth to a boy on 26th May 1972 at Sandylands.

The phone at the side of the bed rang and when Sophie picked it up a man's voice said.

'Good afternoon, is that Mrs Martin?'

Sophie said,

'Yes, it is. Is this Mr Bradshaw?'

The man replied that it was, and he would be happy to see her now if she could come down to the office near the reception desk. Sophie thanked him and said she would be straight down.

Mr Bradshaw was a short man, about fifty years old. As she entered the office, he introduced himself, offering his hand in greeting and gesturing for her to take a seat in front of the desk. He began the conversation by asking if she'd come far. Sophie was impatient to get down to business, but politely answered that she had only come from her home in Bath that morning.

'So, what can I do for you Mrs Martin,' he asked finally.

Sophie launched into an explanation of why she was here. Out of respect for her mother she didn't go into too much detail, simply saying that she was trying to trace a baby who, she believed, had been born at Sandylands in 1972 but it seemed may have subsequently been adopted. To get any further with her search she first needed to verify that the time and date of his birth, and the birth name she had for him was correct. In order to do this, she needed, if possible, to find the written record of his birth and possibly the circumstances surrounding it and any further information that might assist her. She was hoping that maybe somewhere among the files in the attics here at Sandylands, she might find the information she was looking for.

'Well,' said Mr Bradshaw, 'there are plenty of boxes for you to search through, so when you're ready, I'll be happy to show you where they are.'

Sophie thanked him and said,

'Well, the sooner the better Mr Bradshaw, so I'm ready to start right away.'

With that, Mr Bradshaw led her out of the office and retrieved the key for the attic from the receptionist. They climbed the three storeys up to the top of the house until they reached a brown door that looked as if it hadn't been painted for many years. Inside was a large, low room with small dormer windows which didn't let in much light. The whole place was dark and dusty. Mr Bradshaw switched on the single light, illuminating several piles of dusty boxes.

'Well, here they are,' he said to Sophie, who was feeling rather daunted by the prospect of sorting through them all to find the single bit of information she needed to see.

'Crikey!' Sophie exclaimed, 'That's quite a pile!'

'It is,' Mr Bradshaw agreed. 'Are you sure you want to do this?'

'Absolutely, I do,' Sophie replied. 'It is very important to me, Mr Bradshaw.'

'Right then,' he said, 'I'll leave you to it. Here are

the attic keys, so please, just lock up and take them back to reception when you've finished.'

'Of course I will, and thanks for your help,' Sophie replied gratefully.

After Mr Bradshaw had gone, Sophie started to inspect the boxes one by one. There seemed to be three distinct types, which she assumed may have originated from three separate businesses that had used the building over the years. They were mostly fastened up with sticky tape and she didn't really want to start opening up each one. Some had sticky labels on them, and some had marker pen writing on them. One pile in particular interested her as someone had helpfully written dates on the labels. Unfortunately, the dates on these boxes didn't start until 1990, so far too late to be of interest. She decided she would open a box from the pile that looked as though it had been there the longest. Pulling one of the ledgers out of the box, she could see it was obviously a record of 'patients' who had been treated at Sandylands. However, looking at it more closely, it seemed as though it related to elderly patients, as most of the entries ended in the word 'deceased' and their ages were mostly over eighty.

So, Sophie started on the third type of box. Opening one of them up, she again found that it contained ledgers of some kind and a brief scrutiny revealed that this box was more promising. The entries definitely related to mothers and babies. However, in the box she had opened, she couldn't find any that related to the 1970's. As often happens, the ledger she needed was in the last box she opened. Quickly locating the 1972 ledger she thumbed eagerly through the pages until reaching the month of May. Suddenly, there it was, in black and white: Mother's Name: Joan Simons, Date of Birth: 30.07.1954, Date admitted: 12.05.1972, Baby born: 8pm 26.05.1972, (Male) Given Name: Peter (A) Mother discharged: 10.08.1972.

So that was it. She assumed the (A) meant 'adopted'. Her mother had spent three months here, two of them with her little boy, Peter, and had then given him up for adoption. She couldn't begin to imagine how traumatic that was for Joan, or how she could have lived with this terrible secret for all these years without telling anyone.

It occurred to Sophie that Sandylands Home for Mothers and Babies may have actually arranged adoptions for the babies born there, or they may have used a particular adoption agency. It might be worth her while to search through the rest of the boxes from that time, to see if she could find out who Peter was placed with, or at least, where she should go next in her search.

She spent the rest of the afternoon searching through the boxes, but without any further success. She supposed that the information, had it existed, would have been completely confidential and therefore may even have been destroyed when the place was sold to the next owner. She would have to take a further look at the Adoption Register site when she got home. Maybe Peter had already registered on it, in an attempt to find his birth mother. If not, she would use an intermediary to search for him. In any event, there wasn't much more she could find out here. She tidied the boxes then left the loft, locking it up and taking the key downstairs to leave at the reception desk for Mr Bradshaw.

She enjoyed a pleasant dinner, then spent an hour in the bar enjoying a glass of wine, after which she decided on an early night and went up to her room to ring Charles to tell him what she had found out. When she called him, he said they had all had a great day at the beach. The children had spent most of the afternoon in the water and with them happily occupied, he'd had time to chat to his parents for once, which was nice. Sophie told him she would be leaving after breakfast in the morning as there was nothing else she could do at Sandylands, so she would pick them up from the station. She told him to give her a ring when they were on their way, which he agreed to do, before telling her he loved her and saying goodnight.

As she lay in bed her mind was full of pictures of her mother. She felt her pain at giving Peter up. It was almost unbearable to think of her here, maybe in this very room, in such distress. She thought about the countless other young women who had suffered emotional trauma in this place, and it was almost as though the walls had soaked up all that misery, which was now exuding into the atmosphere around her. Eventually she fell into a shallow sleep.

The next morning, after a fitful night, Sophie dragged herself out of bed, washed, dressed, and went down to breakfast, after which she found Mr Bradshaw and thanked him for his help. She settled her bill and then got away nice and early, keen to get home to have an hour or two of peace before Charles and the children needed picking up from the station. She would prepare homemade pizzas – their favourite, with a nice green salad. She also needed to sort out their uniforms for the following day. Just a couple more weeks of school would bring the school holidays. They had booked a cottage in the Yorkshire Dales for two weeks at the beginning of August and she was looking forward to getting away from every-thing, just able to be together, to relax and enjoy the wonderful scenery.

She decided that before they left for Yorkshire she would engage an intermediary to begin the search for Peter. Maybe they would have some news by the time they returned to Bath. She turned all this over in her mind as she drove through the Wiltshire countryside. Her thoughts drifted to her mother. She was begin-ning to feel that she never really knew her. Surely, the person she knew would never have been able to give a baby up for adoption, let alone keep his entire exis-tence a secret from the people closest to her. It was strangely disorientating, when you discover that you didn't even know your own mother, she reflected.

She thought about Grannie Simons. Her mind was

very confused now and Sophie decided it would be cruel to give this information to her yet. Maybe when she found Peter, depending how things turned out, she could introduce him to her, perhaps as a friend. Sophie decided that to let her know that her daughter had had a baby all those years ago without telling her, would be too hurtful. She must go and visit Grannie soon. Sophie wasn't even sure she had understood that Joan was dead. It was so tragic.

It was about twelve o'clock when Sophie parked the car outside the house. She was glad to be home. It felt good to be in her own space again, and to put to one side the unsettling images she had been seeing in her mind's eye for the last day or so, of her mother giving up her baby to strangers. She unpacked, showered, and put on her jeans and jumper then went down to the kitchen and made herself a sandwich and cup of tea, which she took out into the garden. She never tired of the view across the city. She felt privileged to live here and was thankful for all the chances she'd been given in life that had led her to this point. In fact, she thought, what her mother had done all those years ago had probably contributed to the privileged life she had been given. If Joan had brought up the child as a single mother, her life would have been very different and she would probably never have met and married her father, and Sophie herself would never have been born.

Funny how things work out, she mused, it's all

about cause and effect at the end of the day. None of us know what impact the things we do today, will have on people's lives in years to come.

Chapter 9

SUCCESS

Sophie arrived at the station early. She wanted to be on the platform when the train pulled in, needing to see the delight on the children's faces when they saw her waiting for them. Somehow, she needed re-assurance about the strength of her bond with them. Reassurance, she supposed, that she could never have done what her mother had done and being there when they stepped down from the train suddenly seemed important. It was only yesterday she had dropped them off at the station, but it seemed longer. She had visited a different world since then, a rather disturb-ing one full of the ghosts of young women forced by circumstance to give up the most precious thing any woman can hold – her new-born baby.

The train appeared in the distance and she was excited. She had missed them all, even if it had only been for a day. As the train slowly rolled in, they saw her immediately and started waving excitedly from the open window of the carriage door. Then they were racing along the platform and into her arms and she hugged them tight. Charles strode up behind them and joined the group hug. It felt good and Sophie was back in her happy place once more.

As she drove them back up the hill to home, they chattered excitedly about their weekend with Grannie and Grandad, and how they had had two ice creams each, and pushed Dad for miles out to sea on the li-lo and eaten fish and chips on the beach. Sophie listened happily, smiling at Charles who squeezed her hand as it rested on the gear stick.

After their pizza and salad supper in the garden, Charles said it was time they started to plan their trip to the Dales. He felt it would be good to give Sophie something new to focus on for a while and brought the AA book down from the study. They had booked a cottage called Southview where they had stayed before. It was in a hamlet nestling in the shadow of Castle Bolton, overlooking Wensleydale. It was a wonderful part of the world and Charles and Sophie both loved it. They checked on Charles' phone to see what events might be happening in the area, and on the National Trust site to help them to decide where to visit whilst they were up there. However, they both agreed it would be best not to be too organised. They simply needed to relax and unwind after the last few months and Isabella and Henry would be happy just to paddle in the river in the valley and explore the woods. Maybe Charles could take Henry fishing; he would love that, they decided. Charles said he would pick up a small rod for him before they went.

Charles and the children would break up for the summer holiday in a couple of weeks so Sophie would be busy preparing for the trip. They would be away for two whole weeks and she couldn't help her mind returning to her quest and was determined to set the wheels in motion by contacting an adoptee tracing agency the next day. She felt it may take some time before they got anywhere with it, but hopefully by the time they returned from their holiday, they may have some results for her.

Finally, Sophie ushered the children upstairs for their shower to remove the last of the sand from their hair and between their toes. They were allowed to come down for some warm milk and a biscuit before cleaning their teeth, saying goodnight to Charles, and following Sophie back up to their rooms. She tucked them in extra tightly and kissed them both fondly on their foreheads before turning out their lights.

Charles was curious to find out what she was going to do next in her search for Peter. Secretly he hoped she wasn't going to get too obsessed with finding him. For a start, it may not be possible, and if she was able to, he may not be what she was expecting, or he may not even want to know her. She had no idea what his life was like, or indeed, what kind of a person he was. Just because he is her half-brother, he thought, doesn't mean he's going to be anything like her. If he's had a hard life it may have left its mark on him. The last thing Charles wanted was for Sophie to get hurt. He loved her so much, it would be dreadful to watch, if all her good intentions came to nothing, or worse, resulted in bitter disappointment. On the other hand, he knew his wife better than anyone. He was sure she would never be able to let this go. She would not rest until she had found this man. He would just have to be there for her, to join in her happiness if it worked out and to pick up the pieces if it didn't.

When Sophie came down to the kitchen, he asked her how she was feeling about it all now and what was she intending to do next. She told him she was finding it difficult to reconcile the mother she had known with the woman who had given up her baby and apparently been able to dismiss him from her life. Charles pointed out that actually, it was obvious her mother had never forgotten Peter, as she had kept the box containing his photo and clothes all these years. No one would ever know how many times she had taken that box down from the loft to look inside and to remember him. Nor did anyone know what anguish it may have caused her.

Sophie had to admit that he was right. Who was she to judge her mother? She really had no idea what effect it had had on her. All those years, living with this secret, unable to tell her parents, or even, as far as Sophie knew, her husband, and certainly not her child, about it. For the first time she felt real empathy for her mother and what she had gone through and was thankful to Charles for helping her to look at things from this new perspective. She told him she was now going to hand over the search to an intermediary, an adoptee tracing agency, because even if she were able to find him herself, she realised it would be unwise to approach him directly. He may not want to see her, or he may not even be aware he was adopted and finding that out could be shattering for him.

Charles was pleased Sophie had apparently thought this through thoroughly, and once again, he admired his wife's ability to analyse a situation and act in a considered way. He was reassured that she intended to handle this sensitively and told her he thought she was doing the right thing, using an agency.

They discussed Joan's cottage and decided to finally clear the loft on the following Saturday so that Sophie could arrange for the house clearance people to empty the rest of the furniture and effects whilst they were away in Yorkshire.

Fortunately, Sophie managed to arrange a play date for the twins with some school friends, so they could concentrate on the job in hand. In the event it took them all day Saturday to load up the car and all day Sunday to unload it and carry everything up to the spare room at the top of their house. Sophie told herself that one day, she would sort it all out, but for now, it was all safe enough there. It was mainly books and photographs anyway, and they could wait.

She contacted an agency called Family Finders and went along for an appointment. She passed over all the information she had about Peter, which didn't seem very much. However, they were optimistic that, given his birth name and date and place of birth, they should be able to find him. Of course, whether he would want to be contacted was a different matter and she must prepare herself for possible disappoint- ment on that score. She assured them that she had thought this through fully and was prepared for every eventuality.

Southview, Castle Bolton

As Sophie opened the cottage door, the scene that greeted her almost moved her to tears. She felt she had never seen such a beautiful sight. The valley was filled with mist, but here on the hill it was swirling around the ruins of Castle Bolton, whilst the sun was high enough in the sky to bathe the whole scene in golden light. The air was filled with birdsong and she was reminded once again just how much she loved this place. She sat down on the bench under the cottage window to enjoy her early morning cup of tea before the rest of the family appeared, demanding her attention.

Inevitably, her thoughts turned to the search for her brother, and she wondered whether the agency had managed to find out anything so far. She had told them she would be away on holiday for two weeks and would contact them on her return. Although she could have rung them, she had so far resisted doing so, wanting to concentrate on Charles and the children and to simply enjoy some quality time with them. It wasn't easy though. Her mind was constantly drawn back to Peter. What would he be like? Would he want to see her? Where was he living? On and on it went. Now, she physically shook her head to redirect her thoughts, and began to wonder how the house clearance had gone. They should be finished by now and the cottage would be ready to be sold. She decided to contact an estate agent as soon as they got home. It would be strange to see the old place completely empty. Poor mum, she thought and wondered whether she would ever know what had really happened at the hospital that night. It hurt so much that she wasn't even able to say goodbye and give her one last hug.

She was dragged back to the present as Charles appeared at the cottage door with a cup of tea in his hand. He stood for a moment, taking a deep breath, and surveying the scene as Sophie had done.

'I'd almost forgotten how lovely it is here,' he said.

'I know,' Sophie replied, 'so had I.'

He sat down beside her, and they began to think about the day ahead.

'I think we'll pop over to Richmond today,' he said, 'I'm pretty sure it's market day.'

'Sounds good to me,' said Sophie, just as Isabella popped her head out of the doorway, asking when breakfast would be ready. Henry tumbled out behind her, almost knocking her over. To ward off the ensuing row, Sophie offered them pancakes for breakfast, if they would come and help to make them. They readily agreed and half an hour later they were eating their way through a substantial pile.

The days in Yorkshire passed by all too quickly. They had walked, fished, explored the woods and swum in the rivers. It had been wonderful to spend time together, even with Sophie's thoughts frequently returning to matters back home.

The journey home seemed endless. There was quite a bit of holiday traffic around now as it was well into August. Once they left the Dales it was motorway all the way, apart from the last few miles. Sophie and Charles shared the driving and they had frequent stops at the services, to relieve the boredom as much as anything. Thank goodness Isabella and Henry each had their own tablets so they could watch their favourite films to pass the time. Finally, they pulled up outside the house and as always, Sophie surveyed it with pride. She still couldn't believe that she and Charles had managed to get such a wonderful home together. It was too late to start cooking and once they had unloaded their bags, Charles ordered a takeaway from their favourite Thai restaurant.

The next day, a little nervously, Sophie rang the agency to find out if they had managed to get anywhere with the search. The lady who answered took her name and asked her to wait a moment while she put her through to Amelia Frost, the lady who had been dealing with her case.

A bright, young sounding voice said,

'Good morning Mrs Martin.'

Sophie responded politely and then, anxious to get on with things, asked whether she had any information for her.

'Well, it is largely good news. We have located your half-brother and have written to him to ask if he would be willing to meet you. That was a week ago, and so far, we haven't had any reply from him. Unfortunately, until he does respond, we aren't able to give you any details about him.'

Sophie felt that this was, in the main, quite good news. She now knew he was still alive, and that at least someone knew exactly where he was. This made him seem more real, less of a figment of her imagination. However, she was disappointed he hadn't replied immediately. Would he ever respond? Well, that was out of her hands and she would just have to be patient. Amelia promised to let her know the minute anything occurred. If he did respond, she said, the ball would still be largely in his court. If he wanted to meet her, he would be asked to suggest a time and a place and it would be up to her to accept at that point, or not.

Joan's cottage had now been put on the market at an asking price of £425,000 which sounded like an awful lot of money, particularly as her mother had told her they had bought it for just £45,000 in 1979. She rang the estate agent to see if there had been any interest at all. He told her that there had already been three viewings and the responses had been good, although no one had yet put in an offer. He said he would ring her if anyone was seriously interested. This would be a considerable boost to their savings and Sophie wondered what on earth they would do with it. She supposed the wisest thing to do would be to add it to their pension pots, but she felt that at least some of it could be used to pay off part of the mortgage and then take the children to Disneyworld, for which they had been pestering them for ages.

Meanwhile, in his flat in Fishponds, John read the letter from the agency for the fourth time. He supposed he should have expected it, now that woman, as he now thought of her, was dead and buried. Maybe her daughter had found something in the house telling her about him after all. This was so ironic, he almost laughed out loud. He had been kept a secret all his life by that woman and within weeks of her death, all and sundry knew. What a fool she had been. If only she had accepted him, things could have been so different.

Since her death he had been regularly searching through the estate agents' sites. He wondered whether they would be putting that cottage up for sale. It would be interesting to know how much the old girl was worth; how much he might have inherited if things had been different. That very morning his search had revealed that it was now, in fact, on the market for £425,000. My God, he thought, what I couldn't do with a share of that!

Looking again at the letter, which as yet, he hadn't responded to, the thought occurred to him that maybe, just maybe, there was a way he could get his hands on some of it. He calculated that it was likely the old girl hadn't mentioned him before she died, and that this Sophie didn't know about his visit to Corston. If that were the case, he could pretend he had no idea who his mother was or where she lived, and therefore had never met her. When she informed him that his mother was only recently deceased, he would be able to fain his devastation that his mother had died before they could meet, thereby maybe winning her sympathy and who knows, perhaps even a share of the money, which after all, was only his due!

He decided to sleep on it, but the next day, it still seemed to make sense to accept her approaches, and he rang Amelia Frost, the agent who had written to him.

'Hello,' he said, 'It's John West here.'

Amelia Frost sounded pleased to hear from him and replied,

'Ah, Mr West, thank you for getting back to me.'

'Yes, I'm sorry it's taken so long, but it's been a big decision for me,' he explained.

'Please don't apologise,' Amelia replied, 'these things need thinking about carefully. They can be life changing. Have you reached a decision Mr West?'

'I have,' he replied, 'I would like to meet Sophie, my half-sister. I don't know how it will go long term, but I do feel that as she's made the effort to find me, I ought to respond. What is the next step Miss Frost?'

Amelia said that she was pleased he had come to

a decision and that she would now arrange a meeting with Sophie at a time and place to suit him.

'Do you have anywhere in mind, John. Do you mind if I call you that?'

'No, of course not,' he said. 'Does Sophie live nearby?'

'Well, not too far away. She lives in Bath, and I'm sure she'd be happy to come over to Bristol to meet you. I would suggest somewhere quite public for a first meeting.'

'Well, how about the Wetherspoons down on the docks? Do you think that would be ok?'

'Yes, I'm sure that would be perfect. Could you give me a couple of suggestions for the day and time?' Amelia asked him, sounding pleased that things were going so well.

'Does Sophie work?' he asked her.

'I don't believe so,' Amelia answered.

'Well, can I suggest two o'clock on Thursday or Friday next week. I'll be working nights at the hospital so I could have an hour or two to spare either afternoon.'

'That's great, John. I'll get in touch with her and get back to you. Thank you again for ringing. I'm sure we'll speak again soon.'

John said thank you and goodbye and then hung up.

Well, that was it, next week he would meet this Sophie. I wonder how that will go, he thought to himself. What a strange situation, meeting a sister he hadn't known existed until a couple of months ago.

The timing could have been better, he thought, but that was down to that woman.

Amelia rang Sophie immediately, who was of course excited to hear the news that Peter had been in touch. She told her that he was happy to meet her in Bristol and offered her the two times he had suggested. She agreed to see him on Thursday at 2 o'clock. Amelia asked her if she could send a photo of herself that she could pass on to John, as he was now called. Sophie was only too happy and sent one from her phone, then almost ran up the stairs to tell Charles, who was reading in the study.

It seemed like the longest week of Sophie's life.

Chapter 10

THE MEETING

As the week passed, Sophie could hardly think of anything else. She found it difficult to get to sleep. She would soon have the brother she had always longed for. She went through the motions of looking after the children, helping Charles to keep them entertained, doing the usual 'holiday stuff' of taking them swimming, bike riding along the canal, or playing in the park. She wasn't completely 'present' though, talking often about the coming meeting and what it could mean to her.

Charles did his best to dampen her enthusiasm. He was very apprehensive, instinctively knowing that this could affect not only Sophie's life, but also his own. The family dynamics were bound to change, particularly initially, as Sophie dealt with the emotions all this was bound to elicit in her. If he was honest, it had already impacted on their relationship. Since the day she had found out she had a half-brother, Sophie had been preoccupied. He would quite often make some casual remark to her, only to be ignored, and when he looked at her, would see that she was lost in thought. Of course, he knew there was nothing he could do about it. Things would have to take their course. Much would depend on what kind of a person this John was. If he were a decent sort, maybe it would all work out for the best, but who knew what kind of a life he'd had, and what effect it might have had on him?

In their own ways, both Sophie and Charles approached the following Thursday with something akin to dread. It meant so much to Sophie that she was afraid that John would turn out to be nothing like the brother she had always wanted and may not even want to have a relationship with her and her family. As far as Charles was concerned, he fervently hoped that would be the case and that they could put this whole thing behind them and get back to the way they were before.

Sophie decided to take the train over to Bristol. It was a cloudy day with a light breeze as she walked down to the station, past the cricket ground. Charles was at home with the children as it was the last week of their summer holidays. She was feeling nervous but happy at the same time. As she walked, she thought about her mum. Would she be glad that she had found 'Peter'? She felt sure she would. It can't have been easy, carrying that guilty secret all those years.

Arriving at the station she bought her ticket,

walked through the tunnel, and climbed the stairs to the Westbound platform. The train was due in five minutes and she sat on a bench to wait. She decided she would walk to the docks from the station, which would take about twenty-five minutes or so. The train was fairly busy as always, but she managed to find a window seat and settled down to enjoy the views of the Avon valley for the fifteen minutes or so it would take to reach Bristol Temple Meads station.

Stepping down from the train, she glanced at the station clock. It was 1.30, which meant she just had half an hour to walk over to Wetherspoons where she would meet John. She had decided to dress casually in jeans and a tee shirt with a casual denim jacket over it. She had of course made an effort with her hair and makeup. This may be one of the most important meetings of her life and she didn't want to let herself down. It was with some trepidation that she arrived at the docks. She could see Wetherspoons on the other side of the river and her heart skipped a beat. She paused for a moment, then took a deep breath and strode across the bridge.

Meanwhile, John had been making his own way down to the docks. He also felt that this meeting was going to be one of the most important of his life, but for slightly different reasons. Just a few months ago he would have been happy to be meeting his sister. He too had always wanted brothers and sisters, but unfortunately, it was too late for happy families now. He glanced at the time on his phone. It was 1.45. He had wanted to be there early so that he could observe Sophie as she arrived. Amelia Frost had sent him a photo of her so that he would be able to recognise her. As Amelia hadn't asked him for a photo, he assumed Sophie wouldn't know what he looked like. He chose a table by the window so he could see her as she approached. Just before two, he saw her striding across the bridge over the river. She looked younger than he had expected, about thirty, he guessed. She was blonde and rather attractive in a down to earth sort of way. As she entered the pub he stood up and smiled at her, so that she would realise who he was. Sophie saw him immediately and it was obvious from his demeanour that this must be John, her brother. He stretched out his hand as she approached, saying.

'Hello Sophie, it's great to meet you at last.'

Sophie felt a bit awkward, not knowing how familiar to be with him. She had imagined they might give each other a hug, but now the moment had arrived, it didn't seem appropriate. There was a certain restraint in his manner that precluded any sort of intimacy of that sort. Consequently, Sophie just smiled and took his hand.

'John, I'm so glad you agreed to meet me. Thank you so much.' she blurted out.

John had already got himself a drink before she arrived, but now asked her if she would like something.

'A lager would be nice, thanks,' she replied, and he went over to the bar to get her one.

She observed him standing at the bar and thought,

so that is my brother. He was nothing like she had imagined him to be. She had thought he would probably be some kind of professional. Maybe he would be a teacher, or a doctor, or maybe a solicitor. Well perhaps he is, she thought, appearances can be deceptive. As it was, although he was clean and tidy, she could see that his clothes suggested that they had been well worn and his trainers were obviously from a supermarket. She wasn't a snob, but she knew quality when she saw it, and clothes can say a lot about a person.

He came back with her drink and sat down in front of her. In that awkward way that sometimes happens when strangers meet, they both started to speak at once, neither of them quite sure where to begin.

Sophie spoke first.

'Please, do go on.'

John started speaking again, saying how pleased he was that she had contacted him. He said he'd had no idea that he had a sister, or was it a half-sister, he asked.

'Well,' Sophie replied, 'As far as I know, you are my half-brother.'

'Right,' he said. 'Well, I've known I was adopted since I was ten years old, but had no idea how or why that happened, or who my real mum was.'

'That must have been awful for you,' Sophie responded in a caring tone, which caught him by surprise. He wasn't used to people caring about his feelings these days.

'It was,' he stated in a matter-of-fact way which conveyed much meaning to Sophie, who was already feeling sorry for this man in front of her who looked as though he had been denied the privileged life she had had.

'I've got so many questions to ask you,' he went on, 'What about our mother, is she still alive? Are there any more of us?'

Sophie looked down at the table, unable to speak for the moment. She looked up at him and he was actually touched by the concerned expression on her face, sorry for a moment that he had decided to put her through this, but it was too late now.

'John,' she said, and he noticed she had tears in her eyes as she went on, 'I'm terribly sorry to have to tell you, that Joan, our mother, passed away a couple of months ago.'

'No! How? What happened to her?' he asked quickly, with a look of disbelief on his face.

Sophie explained about the operation and the sudden death of their mother, for which they still hadn't been given a satisfactory explanation, as the post-mortem hadn't revealed an obvious cause.

'I don't know what to say,' John continued, 'that must have been awful for you and the rest of the family. I have to say, I'm gutted. For so long, I've dreamt of meeting my own mother, and to find out now that I am just too late – well, I just can't believe it. But tell me, why didn't you try to find me earlier. Did you not know about me?'

'John, I'm sorry,' Sophie replied, 'but I didn't know you existed until I went through Mum's things and found a box with your photo as a tiny baby and some of your baby clothes in it.'

'You mean, she never told you about me?' he asked in an incredulous tone. 'Did anyone know?'

'I don't think so,' Sophie replied softly.

John was shocked that his mother had in fact kept his photo and baby clothes. So, she hadn't forgotten him after all. He fell silent, obviously deep in thought, and Sophie thought it best to allow him time to digest what she had just told him. Eventually, he looked up and asked her again,

'So, you don't know why she gave me up? Was she very young? Was she on her own?'

'Well, as far as I can work out, she would have still been at Manchester University. She was twenty. Her father was in the Diplomatic Corps and I imagine they would have been overseas at the time. I guess that's why she didn't tell them. Being still at Uni, she wouldn't have any income of her own I suppose and to keep you she would have had to leave Manchester.'

'So, do we have any other brothers or sisters?'

'No, there's just us John. I always wanted siblings, but Mum couldn't have any more after me, so I grew up alone. What about you, were you an only child too?'

'I was, and I too was desperate for a brother or sister. Ironic isn't it, that we both grew up alone when in fact we had a sibling not a million miles away. Where did you grow up, in fact?'

'In Corston, near Bath,' she replied, 'do you know it?'

'I've heard of it,' he said, 'I grew up in Bristol, so just about, what, ten miles away?'

'Well, we've found each other now,' Sophie said, 'and I would like to get to know you better, if you'd like that too.'

'I would, definitely,' John replied, 'I don't want to lose you now Sophie.' And he meant it.

They carried on chatting quite amiably. John asked her about her family and seemed pleased that he had a niece and a nephew, saying he hoped he would get to meet them soon. Sophie said she would like that, and then asked him about his own family. He told her the whole sorry tale about his own marriage and the fact that his children were now living halfway across the world. He didn't, of course tell her about his rather colourful life before meeting Julie. Sophie felt sorry for him and said she couldn't imagine how awful it must be for him to lose his children. In Sophie's eyes this explained a lot about the air of sadness, and yes, a little self-neglect that he had about him. He was short of someone to care about him, that much was obvious, she thought to herself. He told her that he was working for a cleaning company, but that was only temporary until he could find something better. It was obvious to Sophie that his life was very differ-ent from her own and she couldn't help feeling a little guilty about that. How different might his life have turned out if her mother hadn't given him away, she wondered.

Well, maybe she would be able to make amends for some of that, by getting to know him and welcoming him into her own family. They seemed to be getting on well and the conversation flowed easily. After an hour or so, Sophie looked at her watch and said she would have to go. She needed to catch the four-thirty train to Bath. John said he needed to go anyway as he was on the night shift tonight at the hospital. Sophie asked him for his address saying she would drop him a line in a week or two to arrange for him to come over to Bath to meet her family. He said he would look forward to that. He walked with her as far as the bridge over the river, then they shook hands, still rather formally, and parted.

As John strode up the hill to home, he was congratulating himself on pulling off the necessary deception pretty well. He didn't think that Sophie would have guessed he'd already met her mother. Sophie actually seemed very nice. Obviously, she had been well brought up by his mother. She was kind and sensitive and he had enjoyed talking to her. What a pity they hadn't met just a few short months ago, but there it was. Can't turn the clock back now, he thought.

For her part, Sophie thought the meeting had gone pretty well. John seemed a genuine sort although she suspected he had quite a back-story somewhere. He seemed too intelligent to settle for being a hospital cleaner, although he had said it was only temporary. She thought he took the news about her mother rather well, but then he had never even met her, so she couldn't expect him to be grief stricken, could she? He had been easy to talk to and something about his eyes reminded her of her mother. He definitely had one or two of her mannerisms, such as the way he tilted his head to one side when listening to her, and when he smiled, the way his mouth turned up slightly more at one side than the other. These were just little things, but enough to make him seem familiar to her and she had definitely warmed to him as they talked. She looked forward to him visiting them in Bath in a couple of weeks. She was sure Charles wouldn't mind her inviting him, because he knew how much this meant to her.

Sophie arrived home about five thirty. Charles was in the kitchen preparing supper. He called out to her as she closed the front door.

'Hi love, I'm down here.'

She clattered down the stairs into the kitchen, then walked over and kissed him on the cheek.

'What did I do to deserve that?' he asked.

'Oh, I don't know,' she replied, 'just being here,' and kissed him again.

He slipped his arm around her waist and gave her a long lingering kiss.

'Wow, I should go away for the day more often,' she murmured.

'Don't you dare,' he said, and then added. 'Anyway, how did it go?'

'It went pretty well, I think,' she said.

'You don't sound too sure,' he replied.

'Well, it was good, really, but he wasn't anything like I expected him to be.'

'How do you mean?' Charles asked her.

'I don't know. I thought he might be a professional type, you know, a teacher like you, or a solicitor or something.'

'And wasn't he? What does he do then?' he enquired.

'Well, he said it's only temporary but he's working for a cleaning company at the moment.'

'Oh, I see what you mean.'

'He does seem really bright though, so it seems like there might be some sort of a history there somewhere. Anyway, we chatted easily for an hour or so, and I would like to see him again soon. In fact, I've invited him over for lunch one day in a couple of weeks. I said I'd drop him a line in a day or two to arrange it. You don't mind, do you?'

In spite of his reservations, Charles knew it would be no use objecting at this stage and said that of course he didn't mind and would be glad to meet him. In fact, he thought to himself, the sooner I can give this guy the once over, the better.

Just then, the twins came clattering and jumping down the three flights of stairs from their rooms in search of food. Charles had just finished cooking the rice and chilli and served it up. As she sat eating her supper, Sophie thought how lucky she was to have this wonderful family around her, and then she thought of John, probably eating his supper alone. Why should she have had everything, and he had nothing, because of matters completely outside his control. Life just doesn't seem fair sometimes, she thought.

Chapter 11

BATH

A week later, as John returned home from his day shift, he picked up a letter that had been placed in his post-box down in the hallway. He took it up to his room, made himself a cup of tea and sat down to open it.

It was from Sophie. In the letter, she said how nice it had been to meet him, and it would be lovely if he would come over for lunch the following Sunday. Her husband Charles was looking forward to meeting him, and they would probably have a barbecue in the garden if the weather was good. Sounds nice and middle class, John thought to himself. Barbecue in the garden eh? Still, it was good of her to invite him and he would of course be going. It would certainly be interesting to see how the other half lives, he thought.

He picked up his phone and dialled the number

she had given him. It rang quite a while before she answered.

'Hello, Sophie Martin here,' she said.

'Hello Sophie, it's John,' he answered.

'Oh, hi John,' Sophie replied cheerfully, 'Sorry I took so long to answer, I was upstairs in the study.'

In the study, he thought, nice for some!

'Oh, that's ok,' he said, 'I just got your letter, thank you. I'd love to come and meet your family.'

'That's great John.'

'What time do you want me?' he asked.

'Oh, shall we say around one o'clock?' Sophie said tentatively.

'Yes, that'll be fine. Could you text me your address? I'll be coming on the train from Bristol. Is it far from the station?'

'Not really, about a ten-minute walk. Will you be ok, I could pick you up,' she offered.

'No,' said John, 'that's fine, the walk will do me good, and it will be nice to see a bit of Bath on the way.'

'OK then, well, if you get lost, give me a ring.'

'I will, so I'll see you next Sunday at about 1 o'clock.'

He had to admit to a certain nervousness. He would have to be on his guard not to reveal anything that might arouse her suspicion. He reminded himself that she knew nothing of his visit to Corston and on no account was she to find out about it. He wondered what Charles was like. A professional type, I shouldn't wonder, he thought. I must be prepared for some quizzing from that quarter. He would have to be on his toes alright and he thought for a split second that perhaps he was foolish to get involved with the family at all. Then he remembered the money and told himself not to be such a nerd.

The following Sunday, John caught the twelve o'clock train from Bristol. He had never had much call to visit Bath over the years. It seemed like a world that had never been meant for the likes of him. However, as he walked along the road from the station now, past the Abbey and the river, and then along a wide boulevard lined with Georgian terraces with an imposing pilastered building in the distance, he had to admit that it was a beautiful place. Quite an eye opener, actually. It was nothing like Bristol. It had been built to a plan hundreds of years ago, and little had changed since then. At least, not around here, he thought.

Checking the map on his phone he could see he was about ten minutes away from the address Sophie had given him and had a few minutes to spare. He took a short detour along the side of the canal, and sat down on a bench on the towpath, to take in the view of the city spread out below. At precisely one o'clock he stood up and walked along to the bridge over the lock then climbed the short, steep hill towards the road where Sophie lived.

He turned left at the top of the hill and strode along

the road, checking the numbers as he went. Finally, he arrived at number 24. He squared his shoulders, took a deep breath, and rang the doorbell. He could hear the clatter of children's feet coming down the stairs, each of them shouting that they would get it, followed by

'I will!'

'No, I will!'

Then the door opened, and Charles was there, smiling.

'Ah, you must be John,' he said.

'Yes, and you must be Charles.'

'I am,' Charles replied, holding out his hand in greeting, 'Please, come in.'

The two children he had heard arguing were standing in the hall, one each side of their father. John smiled down at them, saying,

'I'm John, and you are Henry and Isabella, is that right?'

They both smiled up at him, then Charles said quickly,

'Come on then, let's go find mummy.'

With that, he led the way down the stairs to the family room.

John followed Charles and the children down to the lower ground floor, where Sophie was waiting to greet him.

'John, it's lovely to see you,' she said, coming forward to offer him her hand, 'thank you so much for coming.'

In spite of himself, he was pleased to see her. He definitely felt a connection to Sophie, even though he had warned himself not to get too close to her. Not the way things were now. Just a few weeks ago it could have been so different, he thought. He smiled and shook her hand.

'Lovely spot you've got here,' he said, 'and I never realised how beautiful Bath is. I've never had much cause to come here before.'

'It is,' Sophie replied, 'we love it, don't we Charles?'

Charles agreed enthusiastically and then offered John a drink. Alarm bells rang in John's head. He mustn't disgrace himself by over-indulging, and once he started drinking, often he couldn't stop. He declined alcohol and said that he'd love a cup of tea.

'I'll make us all a cup,' Charles offered, 'why don't you all go into the garden and I'll bring it out there.'

Sophie led John into the garden, and they sat down at the table under the umbrella shade. She called to the children to come outside to get some fresh air and to bring some toys to play with. Henry carried out his Lego box and Sophie brought her book as usual. John was marvelling at the view across the city, and glancing back at the house behind him, he thought that was no less spectacular.

'You've got a lovely home, Sophie,' he said, and genuinely meant it.

To his surprise he felt no envy as he said that. There was something about Sophie that soothed him. She was so genuine and caring, in fact, just the qualities he had been hoping to find in her mother. As his thoughts turned to her and what he'd done, his stomach churned and for the first time, he felt a flash of remorse.

Charles appeared, carrying a tray with the mugs of tea and a plate of biscuits and squash for the children. Placing it on the table he told John to help himself to a biscuit. Without thinking, John replied that he wouldn't have one thanks, as he had to watch what he ate as he was diabetic.

'Sorry to hear that,' said Sophie with concern in her voice. 'Is it severe?'

'Quite,' John replied, 'Type 1.'

Damn, he thought, he hadn't intended to say anything about that. There might be a possibility, however remote, that someone may make the insulin connection at some point in the future.

'That can be quite bad can't it?' Sophie asked.

'Well,' replied John, 'it's not too bad if I keep it under control.'

Henry appeared at the table with his box of Lego and asked John if he'd like to play with him. He wanted to build a spaceship but needed some help. Glad of the distraction from the conversation about diabetes, John enthusiastically agreed, and they set about building the Star Ship Enterprise.

Sophie watched them fondly, pleased that Henry had apparently taken to his new uncle. Charles wasn't quite so pleased. He wasn't sure what to make of John yet. As Sophie had said, he seemed a bright chap, too bright to be working as a cleaner. He needed to know more about his background before he could make up his mind about him.

'Sophie tells me you're living in Bristol, John?' he asked.

'Yes, I am,' he replied.

'I know Bristol pretty well, I used to work in a school there. Whereabouts are you living?'

'Oh, I have a flat in Fishponds. Not brilliant but it suits me for now.' John responded. 'Are you in teaching then?' he went on.

'Yes, I've been teaching since I left Uni.'

'He's just taken over as Head at St Mark's Primary, but he's too modest to say,' Sophie said proudly, smiling fondly at Charles.

'Was that something you always wanted to do?' John asked Charles.

'Well, at one time I thought I might go into medicine, but in the end, I couldn't fancy all those years of training. What about you?'

'Well, from being a little boy I too dreamed of being a doctor, but I'm afraid I never got much of an education, one way or another,' he confided, sadly.

Sophie could see the sadness in his eyes. Her heart went out to him. He seemed full of regrets.

John wondered what it was about this family that was making him open up so much. He would normally never show what he was feeling, let alone talk about his early life. He would have to be more careful. He had too many secrets never to be told.

The spaceship was finished, and Henry ran off to fly it around the garden. Isabella spied her chance and trotted up to John with her book, asking him if he would read to her. John gladly agreed, pleased once again for the conversation to be steered away from himself. Being around these children also reminded him of James and Abigail. It felt good, but he wondered sadly how they were doing. Julie used to send him photos in the beginning, but she hardly ever wrote to him these days.

Sophie was feeling happy that John, her brother, was here and that the children seemed to be taking to him. She still had the feeling that there was a lot more to learn about him, but where's the hurry she thought to herself. Now that we've found each other, we've got a lifetime to get to know one another.

She suggested to Charles that he could light the barbecue, while she went inside to prepare the salad and sort out the burgers for the children and steaks for them. John glanced up as Charles dragged the gas barbecue out of the shed, and the thought occurred to him that this family was short of nothing. This must be what it's like to have a decent job with a regular income. Everything about this family, this place, this house, filled him with regrets for all the things he had never had, and now, would never have.

They all enjoyed the barbecue, and on the surface, the rest of the afternoon was a great success. Sophie was happier than she'd been since her mum had died. She really felt a connection to John and the children seemed to accept him as a new uncle, who was happy to play with them. Charles, on the other hand, still had reservations about him. He felt there was much more to John than he was willing to admit. He said hardly anything about himself. At forty years old or so, he must have had much that he could have told them. He had told Sophie that he had been married and did have two children in Australia, but apart from that he had given little away about his life. He and Sophie on the other hand, had opened their home to him and given him access to their children, who already seemed to be forming a bond with him, which made Charles distinctly uncomfortable.

John had stayed until four o'clock and then left to catch his train back to Temple Meads. After he left, Charles asked Sophie how she felt the afternoon had gone. She seemed very happy and he could see that she meant it. He mentioned his misgivings about John, but this only served to make her angry.

'Well, I think you should give him a chance,' she countered, 'he's obviously not had any of the advantages we've had, and yes, I do feel a bit guilty about that. He should have been growing up with mum and sharing my life. It's not his fault none of that happened. That's down to mum, I'm afraid.'

Wow, thought Charles, that was quite a speech, and felt it best to let the matter drop for now. Sophie had surprised herself with the vehemence of her reply to Charles. Not for the first time she was amazed at the level of emotion this reunion was arousing in her. However, if she was honest with herself, she had begun to wonder slightly that John had, as yet shown little interest in her mother. He had never asked her what she had been like, where she had lived, what did she do for a living; none of that. He hadn't even asked to see a photo of her. Surely, he should be curious to at least find out what she looked like. Then she thought that perhaps he was still angry with her for abandoning him and had decided that he didn't want to know anything about her. Maybe as time went on, this would all become much clearer.

For the moment though, Sophie was more than happy to keep this connection going and had suggested that perhaps she and Charles and the children might go over to Bristol in a week or two. They had been promising Isabella and Henry that they would have a trip to Bristol on the train and then to take them on the ferry to see the SS Great Britain. John, after only a moment's hesitation, happily agreed to meet them and after explaining which shifts he would be working for the next couple of weeks, asked Sophie to text him the details when they had them.

Sitting on the Bristol train, John reflected on the events of the afternoon. His emotions were all over the place. Sophie and Charles had made him so welcome, and the children, his nephew and niece, he reminded himself, were delightful and had seemed to fully accept him as their new uncle. He had never in his life been treated with such unconditional kindness, except perhaps by Alison Greaves, his mentor when he left the Young Offender's institution. But this was different. These people were actually his family, and they had accepted him as such. But if they knew what he had done, all this would end. Sophie would never forgive him, of course, and he was surprised how much that mattered to him.

When he got back to the flat, he checked his sugar levels and realised he needed to inject. This was such a familiar procedure that he could do it blindfolded. This time though, as he inserted the needle something happened. He had a sudden flash back to that night, the night he had injected his mother, which was accompanied by a surge of remorse. This was the second time he'd had this feeling and he knew it was something to do with Sophie. She was awakening something in him that he'd never had before, a feeling of connection. With that came the thought that if he had given her a chance, maybe their mother could have accepted him, but that maybe he hadn't given her that chance. This was a most uncomfortable train of thought and he quickly diverted himself to getting ready for his night shift at the hospital.

Chapter 12

S.S. GREAT BRITAIN

Two weeks later he received a text from Sophie saying that they would be over in Bristol on the coming Saturday, and would he be able to meet them off the ten thirty train from Bath. He texted back to say that he would be happy to and was looking forward to seeing them all again. He was a bit concerned about his finances. He knew that a visit to the SS Great Britain was going to be expensive, but he didn't want to put any obstacles in the way of seeing them again.

As he walked down to the station that morning John gave himself a stern talking to. He really could not get close to these people, he told himself. How could he? After what he'd done just a few short weeks ago, his relationship with them could never lead to anything permanent. How could it? And yet, when he'd received Sophie's letter inviting him to spend the day with them, he couldn't bring himself to refuse. He yearned for the closeness of the real family he'd never known, apart from with Julie and the children of course, but now they were gone. Sophie had accepted him as her brother without question and he had found this unexpectedly moving.

The family arrived on Platform 3 at Temple Meads Station at 10.30 and John was waiting there for them. Isabella and Henry saw him, and he smiled broadly as they ran up to him. This time, Sophie greeted him with a light kiss on the cheek which surprised but delighted him. Charles shook his hand rather coolly, he felt. Maybe, John thought, he still had some work to do to win him over. It wasn't surprising after all, that he would be suspicious of another male interacting with his household, including his children.

They walked to the ferry stop on the river round the corner from Temple Meads. The children were excited by the prospect of a trip on the river and a visit to a sailing ship. Henry said it would be like being a pirate and started slashing around with his imaginary cutlass. Isabella wanted to know would the ship go sailing out to sea.

Charles asked John if he'd ever visited the SS Great Britain.

'Well, I always meant to,' John replied, 'but somehow never got around to it.'

Could never afford to more like, he thought to

himself. He'd wanted to take James and Abigail many times, but never had the cash to spare.

'Well, we haven't been for ages,' Sophie said, 'We came a couple of times years ago, but never since we've had the children, so we're looking forward to showing it to them.'

It was a sunny day, with a brisk breeze blowing over the water as they sailed along the river towards the docks. John, in spite of his misgivings about getting too close to them, felt happy to be with Sophie and her family. After about ten minutes they arrived at the landing stage with the masts of the sailing ship towering into the sky. When they entered the booking hall, Charles strode up to the desk and asked for tickets for three adults and two children. John immediately took out his wallet to give Charles the money for his ticket, but Charles insisted that it was his treat, as they had invited him along.

This family never cease to amaze me, John thought to himself. He wasn't used to such spontaneous generosity. The lady on the desk gave the children a quiz sheet and a pencil each for them to fill in as they explored the ship, designed to help them to learn all about it. As they progressed through the exhibition area and then into the ship itself, Sophie and Charles were kept busy helping Isabella and Henry to find the answers to the clues in their quizzes. The exhibits and the stories behind them were varied and detailed and John found himself absorbed in the history of the ship. He completely lost himself in them until he came to the one about the journeys to Australia it had undertaken in the nineteenth century, which brought him back to the present with a jolt, remembering Abigail and James thousands of miles away. His mood changed and he suddenly thought, what on earth am I doing here? Where do I think all this is leading? I can't go on playing happy families with these people after what I did.

He quickly found Sophie and Charles and the children, and telling them that he wasn't feeling too well, said that he would have to leave. Sophie looked hurt but said, of course, if you're not well, you must go. The children were disappointed as he said goodbye, and even Charles seemed genuinely sorry that he was leaving.

He strode away from the ship feeling upset and angry with himself. For the first time, he truly began to regret what he'd done. Being with Sophie and her family genuinely made him happy. He hadn't felt like that for so long, and yet the memory of that night at the hospital always rose up in his mind to ruin everything. He walked all the way back to his flat and he was determined that he must break all ties with Sophie. He couldn't live this double life and he could never undo what he'd done. By the time he climbed the stairs to his room he had sunk into a black mood, despairing that he could ever escape this place and the life he was living. It was hopeless to even try.

For the next couple of weeks, he went through the

motions of working, eating and sleeping. He tried hard to put Sophie out of his head, but his thoughts always came back to her. Gradually, as the days passed and he thought about the hurt he had caused her, he began to realise that he could never take any share of the inheritance from her mother, as he had originally plotted to do. No, she would be better off without him in her life.

After the trip to Bristol, Sophie had felt confused. She wasn't sure whether John had actually been ill that day. He'd seemed perfectly fine earlier, chatting with the children, and obviously enjoying the trip along the river. She wondered what had changed as they were going through the ship. She wasn't sure what to do next. Had he changed his mind about getting to know them better?

For a few weeks she did nothing, busying herself with the humdrum business of daily life. Then one day she picked up the guidebook they had bought at the SS Great Britain exhibition and was idly scanning through it when a thought struck her. The ship had made regular trips to Australia. That was it! John must have seen that and maybe that was what had upset him, bringing thoughts of his children and, looking at our two enjoying every minute, maybe it was all too much for him. He had just wanted to get away. She put this to Charles, who predictably, thought she was just making excuses for him. He hadn't believed for one minute that John had actually been ill, and it had just confirmed to him that he was an unknown quantity, and he would be quite happy if he never saw him again.

Sophie knew she couldn't just give up on John. She instinctively felt that he was sad and lonely and as his only blood relative, he needed her. She decided she would contact him again. Maybe he would like to meet Grannie Simons, her mum's mother. Not being able to have met his mother must have been a cruel blow, but he could still meet his grandmother, even though she may not be able to understand who he was.

She wrote to John, asking him if he would like to visit Grannie Simons at the nursing home in Bristol where she was living, and if so, she would pick him up and they could go together. John was now in a quandary. His whole being was yearning to see Sophie again, and the prospect of meeting his own grandmother was something he was finding hard to resist, in spite of his misgivings and his previous decision to back away from Sophie and her family. He decided to sleep on it.

The next day he knew he wasn't strong enough to resist Sophie's invitation to see her and to visit his birth grandmother. The urge to meet her was too strong. Sophie had told him that she had dementia and would not understand who he was, but all the same, he needed to see her. It would be difficult of course, to meet the mother of the person he had killed, but it was almost as though he needed to punish himself by seeing her. He was beginning to feel he should be punished somehow. Since he'd met Sophie, little by little he had begun to realise just what a terrible thing he had done. He had deprived her of the mother she loved, and the children of their grandma. It was almost as though he was emerging from a nightmare and couldn't believe he could have done such a thing. The all-consuming anger he had been feeling at the time, had been transformed into remorse by Sophie's acceptance of him and the kindness she had shown him. If only he could turn the clock back.

He rang Sophie and they arranged for her to pick him up outside the flat at mid-day on the following Tuesday. He looked forward nervously to Tuesday, unsure how it would go and how he would react to meeting his birth grandmother, in the circumstances.

Sophie drew up just before twelve and decided to sit in the car outside the flat to wait for John to emerge. While she was waiting, she looked around, trying to get a feel for the neighbourhood. It had once been a grand road but was now pretty run down. All the houses seemed to have been converted into flats, and by the neglected state of them, probably rented out by unscrupulous landlords. John emerged after a few minutes and got into the car.

'Hi,' she said, 'It was a pity you had to miss most of the Great Britain trip. Are you feeling ok today?'

John seemed a little uncomfortable and looked out of the window as he replied,

'Oh yes, I was sorry about that. I felt I needed to get home to check my sugars, I was feeling a bit strange. In the event I was fine. I just have to be careful.

Normally I carry my insulin with me, but I had forgotten it that day.'

'Well, I'm really glad you decided to come and meet Grannie. I'd like to say she'll be thrilled to meet you but as you know she's in the later stages of dementia. To avoid confusing her even more, would you mind if I introduced you as a friend?'

'No, of course not,' John replied.

After ten minutes or so they pulled up at The Grange, a nursing home for the elderly. It was a double fronted Edwardian building, obviously once a large private house but now converted into a nursing home. John followed Sophie up the steps to the front door where she rang the bell. After a few moments, a young lady she hadn't met before opened the door and invited them in.

'Hi,' said Sophie, cheerfully, 'I'm here to see Mrs Simons.'

'Yes, of course,' the young lady replied. 'She's in her room. I'll show you up there.'

Sophie and John followed her up to a room on the first floor. Grannie Simons was sitting in an armchair staring out of the window and didn't even look round when they entered the room. They pulled up chairs and sat down opposite her.

When John looked her full in the face, he was struck by the similarity between her and his mother. She had the same blue eyes and wavy hair, even though hers was white, not brown like his mother's. He found himself trembling with emotion and Sophie immediately noticed the effect seeing Grannie was having on him. She thought it was because he had felt an immediate connection to her, completely unaware of course, of the real reason for his reaction.

'Are you alright?' she asked him.

'Oh, yes, of course, it's all just a bit emotional for me, you know.'

'Of course, I understand.'

Thank God you don't, he thought to himself.

'Grannie, this is my friend John.'

Mrs Simons turned her vacant stare towards him, and suddenly a smile broke out on her face, and astonishingly, she muttered 'Peter' and stretched out her hand towards him.

Sophie was amazed. She had hardly spoken for months, but now she had said his name – his given name. Then she remembered that her grandad had been called Peter. Joan had obviously named her baby after her father.

'She thinks you're Grandad Simons,' she told John, 'his name was Peter, and you must look like him.'

John was shaken. He took the hand she offered, and she squeezed it tightly. She was smiling at him with an expression that could only be described as one of love. Emotion flooded through his body and tears filled his eyes. He had never felt like this before, never felt surrounded by pure unconditional love like this in all his life.

Sophie was moved to tears herself to see the effect John was having on Grannie. Seeing him had touched her soul and reached deep into her mind to bring to the surface emotions and memories that had long been buried under the cloak of dementia. It was wonderful to witness.

John didn't speak. He had no words to express what he was feeling. He simply sat, holding her hand. Neither Sophie nor John wanted to break the spell of this precious moment for Grannie, where she felt, just for a brief time, that she was back with her beloved husband, Peter, and they sat like that, in silence, for a full five minutes or more.

Eventually, the memories must have faded because Mrs Simons looked away from John and towards Sophie, the smile fading from her face, then she snatched her hand away and was gone into her own world once more.

They stayed with her for half an hour or so and Sophie talked to her about their holiday in Yorkshire and about the children and what they had been up to lately. At one point, Grannie seemed to be trying to say Joan, but couldn't form the word, and Sophie tried once more to tell her that Joan had passed away. Grannie said nothing but a tear formed in the corner of her eye and trickled down her cheek. John was mortified, looking down at the carpet wishing it would swallow him up.

What have I done? He kept asking himself, over and over. But he knew all too well what he had done. He had killed her only daughter, his own mother, and he was eternally destined to suffer for it.

As they were driving back to Fishponds, Sophie said,

'That was amazing, I haven't seen Grannie smile like that for years. You really awakened some wonderful memories in her today. Thank you so much for coming, John.'

John was in a state of utter confusion. What he had just experienced was unlike anything he'd felt before. It was as though, holding Grannie Simons hand, there had been a sensation running through his body that could only be described as love. But this was a love he could never accept. He wasn't worthy of it, no more than he was worthy of Sophie's friendship. Unwilling to enter into a conversation with Sophie about what had happened, he just said,

'Yes, it was strange, but I guess she saw the family resemblance.'

Quickly changing the subject and wanting to escape further conversation he suddenly asked Sophie to drop him off at the next roundabout, as he needed to do some shopping on his way home and would walk the rest of the way.

'Oh ok, no problem,' she said, rather surprised, and disappointed that he had chosen to cut their conversation short. She pulled in just after the next roundabout and John quickly said goodbye and jumped out.

He's a queer one, Sophie thought. She had seen how moved he had been by Grannie Simons and she had thought that maybe he would like to talk about it, but it was obvious that he couldn't get away quickly enough when she mentioned Grannie's re-action. Maybe he doesn't really want to be involved with me, she thought sadly. Perhaps she would need to give him some space now and let him make the next move.

Later that evening, when the children were in bed, she explained all that had happened to Charles. He told her that although he had his misgivings about John, he was genuinely sorry that things weren't work-ing out as well as she had hoped and agreed with her that perhaps the next move should come from him.

Chapter 13

INHERITANCE

John, for his part, had decided that he couldn't go on seeing Sophie and her family. It was an impossible situation. However much he was drawn to them, what he had done to her mother had erected an impenetrable barrier between them. He must just accept it and get on with his life, such as it was. So it was, that for the next six months or so, John and Sophie were out of touch, each for their own reasons determined not to contact the other, though they were never far from each other's thoughts.

A deep sadness had descended on Sophie. The grief over her mother's death which in a way had been postponed by her involvement with John, now gripped her once more. It was compounded now by a second grief, that came from realising that not only had she lost her mother, but also it seemed as though she would never have a relationship with her brother.

He had not contacted her since the visit to Grannie Simons, and it looked as though he never would.

As for John, he tried hard to put Sophie out of his mind. He sought to distract himself by frequent visits to the library, when he wasn't working or sleeping. When he was absorbed in a book, he could forget about everything else. For a few hours he could forget he was a murderer. When he was sleeping however, he had no control over the frequent nightmare, which was always the same. He was back in that side ward with his mother, lying there, asleep, and vulnerable. In his dream he prepared the syringe and as he inserted the needle in her arm, she always opened her eyes and they weren't her eyes, they were Grannie Simons eyes, and they were looking at him with unconditional love. He invariably woke up in a cold sweat, often with tears rolling down his cheeks. He felt completely helpless in dealing with this recurring nightmare. If he sought professional help, he would have to reveal what he had done. He began to feel that he was going mad.

By the time March came around, Joan's cottage had found itself a buyer at the asking price. After costs and inheritance tax had been deducted, Sophie received a cheque for £370,000. Even though John didn't seem to want to be part of her life, she still felt that morally he was entitled to at least some of the money and she said so to Charles. He understandably wasn't keen on the idea, given that John seemed indifferent to Sophie's feelings. However, as he said, it was her money, and the decision must be hers. She must do what she felt was right. Consequently, she wrote to John, saying she understood that perhaps he didn't want to develop their relationship any further, but that their mother's cottage had now been sold and she felt he was entitled to a share of it, offering to give him £100,000.

When John read the letter, he moaned out loud,

'No, no, no Sophie!'

He sat with his head in his hands. Was there no end to this torment, he thought to himself. Sophie was offering him more money than he'd ever had in his life, without condition, out of the goodness of her heart and her innate sense of what was right. He knew that after what he'd done, he didn't feel entitled to a penny, but if he refused, from what he already knew about Sophie, she would be deeply hurt and the last thing he wanted to do was to throw her kindness back in her face. He wrestled with the problem for three whole days before reaching a decision.

Trying to forget about Sophie had only made his state of mind worse. The nightmare was as frequent as ever. Maybe Sophie needed this relationship with him. He would have to live with what he'd done whatever happened, so maybe, he reasoned, he ought to accept the money and hope that by getting close to Sophie, helping her and her family whenever and however he could, he would somehow be able to make amends. One thing he did decide though, was that if he were to accept the money, he would have to tell Sophie his whole life story, good and bad, apart from that final act. He wanted to be as honest with her as he could possibly be, short of telling her about her mother's death.

Finally, he rang her, apologising for not being in touch sooner, and explaining that he'd had to do a lot of thinking. He thanked her for her offer of a share of the inheritance and asked if they could meet as he needed to explain something to her before he accepted the money. Sophie was surprised when he rang her. She had expected him to call sooner as it was nearly a week since she had written, offering him the money and by then had thought that he was still ignoring her.

'Yes, of course,' she said, 'I'm more than happy to meet up. Where do you suggest?'

'I'll come over to Bath,' he said. 'Would you mind if I came up to the house? But I would like to speak to you alone, if that's possible.'

'Of course, no problem,' she agreed. The children and Charles are out all day, so if you come for about one o'clock it will give us plenty of time to talk. Is that ok?'

John said that would be perfect and that he would come over on Friday if that was convenient. Sophie said that would be great and looked forward to seeing him then.

When she told Charles that John had rung and had arranged to come over on Friday as he had something he wanted to talk to her about, he wasn't too happy about it.

'What time is he coming?' he asked.

'About one,' she replied.

Charles said he didn't like the idea that she would be there on her own, saying why couldn't he come at the weekend when he would be home.

Ignoring that, Sophie explained that he said he'd been doing a lot of thinking and before accepting the money there was something he needed to explain to her.

'We've always felt he had a back-story, haven't we?' she went on, 'I imagine he wants to fill in the gaps. I admire his honesty, he could have just accepted the money outright, couldn't he?'

Before Charles left for work on Friday morning, he gave Sophie a hug and told her that he hoped it went well, but added,

'Please be careful, love. We really still don't know this man, do we?'

'Well, I hope to know him better after today. Don't worry, I'll be fine,' she reassured him, kissing him lightly on the cheek.

After she had taken the twins to school, she decided to find a few photos of her mother. Surely John would like to have some, she reasoned, as he doesn't even know what she looked like. Maybe it would give her the chance to tell him something about her. He'd never asked, and Sophie wondered why. Also, as the money she was offering him had come from her mother, she felt that, out of respect they should bring her into their conversation today.

She made her way up to the room at the top of the house where she'd stored the boxes from the cottage and gathered together some photos of Joan. Some were taken when she was young, and some more recent ones. She omitted any 'happy family' ones, sensitive to John's possible reaction to them. She went down to the study and put the photos in an envelope, intending to give them to John later.

John was happy at the prospect of seeing Sophie again and was determined to suppress all thoughts of the other matter. When he arrived at her front door, he was feeling very nervous. He was determined to be as honest with her as he possibly could be. How would she react to the fact that he had a criminal record, and had had drug and alcohol problems? She may decide she wanted nothing further to do with him and that he didn't deserve to have any part of the inheritance, and who could blame her? He just didn't know how the next hours would go. He took a deep breath and knocked on the door.

Sophie opened it, welcomed him with a smile and invited him in. Things felt a little awkward after so long, but she led him into the lounge, asking him if he'd like a cup of tea. He said that would be nice and she went down into the kitchen to make it. He looked around the beautifully proportioned room admiringly. He was enjoying the view from the window when Sophie returned with the tea tray and some biscuits.

'It's ok,' she said, 'they're diabetic ones!'

He smiled and thanked her for being so thoughtful.

When they were settled down with their tea and biscuits, Sophie asked him what he wanted to talk about. He hesitated, saying that this wasn't easy for him. She told him to take his time, there was no rush. He explained that since they had met, he hadn't felt able to be completely open with her about his life. He was grateful for her offer of a share of the money but felt that before he accepted it, she should know all about him. He had done things he shouldn't have done and now deeply regretted. His life hadn't been easy, and he wasn't making excuses, but he just wanted to be honest with her and if at the end of it she still wanted to build a relationship with him, he would gratefully accept the money.

Sophie was touched that he should be determined to be honest with her. Since meeting him she had felt there was a lot she didn't know about him. The only part of his life he had talked about was the time he'd spent with Julie. She knew nothing of what had gone before.

John had paused at this point, and Sophie, sensing that he needed some encouragement said,

'John, I'm really touched that you want to be honest with me, it means a lot. Please, go on.'

He launched into the story of his life, beginning with his childhood with his adoptive parents, leaving nothing out, including the violent abuse by his drunken father, and subsequent descent into poverty with his mother. It was hard to tell Sophie about the gang culture he got involved in and the drugs and petty crime, culminating in his detention in the Young Offenders Institution. When he'd finished, he said,

'I'm sorry Sophie, I know this probably isn't what you wanted to hear, but it's important for me to tell you everything, warts and all.'

'I can see this is really difficult for you, and I am truly honoured that you feel you can share it with me. Please, go on.'

When he told her proudly that while in prison, he had been determined finally to come off the drugs, which he had managed to do, she said that must have been so hard for him. He told her about his mentor, Alison Greaves, and she could see how much this lady had meant to him, helping to get him on his feet when even his adoptive mother had rejected him. After the childhood he'd had Sophie was impressed that he had managed to straighten his life out. She could see that he had really tried to make something of himself, even gaining his nursing qualifications, until Julie had let him down and his world had come crashing down once more. Losing his children had been a devastating blow, he told her, and he had begun drinking more than he should, given his medical condition, which resulted in him having to resign from the nursing job he loved. He swore to her - he had now stopped drinking and was ready to sort his life out once more and the money, if she still wanted him to have it, would allow him to do just that.

He had been talking without looking directly at Sophie. It seemed easier somehow, but now he looked up at her and was surprised to see that she had tears in her eyes.

'John, I'm so sorry that life has been so hard for you. You didn't deserve that. Mum should never have given you away. In fact, I have no idea how she could have done that.'

As she spoke, the tears escaped from her eyes and trickled down her cheeks. John was moved, no one had ever cried for him like that, out of sheer concern for what he had gone through. Not even Julie.

'Don't be upset Sophie,' he said quietly, 'none of us know what life will throw at us, we just have to deal with it, and that's what I've tried to do. As you can see, I haven't always made the best decisions, but I've always tried to put things right.'

He couldn't quite suppress the thought that jumped up at him, well, not quite,

Sophie sat quietly for some moments before saying,

'That can't have been easy John. I really respect you for being honest with me. I can see that life has been difficult for you, but I can also see that you've never stopped trying to rise above the setbacks, and that takes courage. As for the money, it makes no difference. That's something I feel you're morally entitled to, and I'm sure mum would want you to have it, given that she was the one who set you on this difficult road.'

John shifted uncomfortably in his seat and then said,

'Thank you for being so understanding Sophie, not

everyone would be.' Then he added, 'You're a very special person, you know.'

A little embarrassed, Sophie explained that since she had known about him, she had been sad that her mother had given him up for adoption and that it was something she was sure she could not have done, not knowing what kind of a life he would have. She went on to say that the course his life had taken was out of his control from the beginning, and she was sorry it had worked out the way it had. Maybe the money would help him to change course for the better now and she was glad she was able to give it to him.

'Well,' he said, 'I've been giving quite a bit of thought to what I would do with the money if you still wanted me to have it. I've decided I'm going to apply to medical school. I know it's a long shot and even if I get in, it's a long road, but I'm determined to try.'

'That would be wonderful!' Sophie exclaimed, 'mum would have been so proud.'

Sophie went on to ask whether he would like to see some photos of Joan. Although right then they were the last things he wanted to see, he forced him-self to say,

'Yes thanks, I would,' with as much enthusiasm as he could muster.

Taking the photos out of the envelope on the coffee table, she handed one to John saying,

'This is mum as she would have been when she had you. She was at Manchester Uni then.'

John looked at the photo without saying a word.

He was thinking plenty of course. This was the young woman in the second graduation photo he'd seen at the cottage. Sophie was looking at him expectantly, and of course he knew why. He should be reacting emotionally to this image of his mother. He was, but it wasn't the emotion Sophie was expecting him to feel. The best he could do was to say how pretty she was, and that Sophie looked like her. Sophie handed him a more recent one, saying,

'This was taken last year, not long before ...,' and he could see that Joan's death was still affecting her.

'She looks like a kind person,' he managed to say.

'She was John, she would have done anything for anyone, and she would have loved you, I know she would.'

This was excruciating for John. He was completely conflicted. Part of him wanted to know more about his mother, as Sophie would be expecting, but his mother was dead; he had killed her, and he certainly didn't want to be thinking about that.

'Thank you so much for showing me these, can I possibly keep them?'

'Yes of course you can,' Sophie answered, putting the photos back in the envelope, thinking that maybe he needed to be alone when he looked at them properly. Perhaps he was finding it too painful; she knew he wasn't good at showing his feelings, like many men.

'Anyway, let's go downstairs, I've made some soup. I hope you've got time to have some with me?'

'Oh, thanks Sophie, that will be great,' he replied, and stood up to follow her down the stairs.

They spent a pleasant hour eating lunch and chatting. John was relieved that he had told her about his past and she hadn't rejected him because of it. They were easy once again in each other's company and it felt good to them both.

Sophie told him that she had the cheque written out for him and popped up to the study to get it. She had put it in an envelope with his name on it and as she handed it to him, she said,

'I hope this will help you to get your life back on track then.'

John stood up, but unable to speak, opened his arms to give her a hug, the first they had had since finding one another.

An hour later John was on the Bristol train and he reflected on the events of the afternoon. For the first time in years, he began to believe that he may have a future. He took the cheque out of the envelope and gazing at it, vowed that he would make every penny count. Determined now to apply to go to medical school and for a mature student loan to cover the fees, he was sure this money would support him for the five years or so it would take him to qualify as a doctor.

As she closed the door behind John, Sophie glanced at her watch. She had an hour before she would need to collect the twins from school and after clearing away the lunch things, went upstairs to the lounge to spend some time thinking about John and what he had told her.

As far as she personally was concerned, she had fully accepted his assurances that the drinking and drugs were firmly in his past, but she knew that Charles may not be so accepting, particularly as he would be hearing it second-hand and couldn't see the sincerity with which John had explained it all. Of course, she knew she would have to tell him but also knew that he would be concerned about the twins, and what influence John might have over them in the future. That was something that did concern her too, and she knew they would have to keep an eye on things in that direction.

When Charles arrived home, he immediately asked how her meeting with John had gone.

'It was fine love,' she assured him. 'Can we talk later,' she added, nodding towards the children.

'Of course,' he said, 'no problem.'

Later that evening while Sophie was settling the twins down upstairs, Charles opened a bottle of Claret and carried it up to the lounge with two glasses. As Sophie came down the stairs, he called to her to join him, pouring them each a glass of wine.

'That's lovely,' she said, kicking off her shoes and relaxing in the armchair. She picked up the glass and went on, 'That's great, just what I needed. It's been quite a day.'

Charles could wait no longer and quickly asked what John had had to say that was so urgent.

Sophie explained that he had said that before he could accept the money, he wanted to be completely honest with her and he would understand if after that, she declined to give him the money, he would understand.

This in itself, impressed Charles greatly. That was quite a risk he was taking. At the same time, he was wondering what was coming. What could be so bad that John thought Sophie may not want to give him the money once she'd heard it?

Sophie took a drink of her wine then began to relate the story of John's life, 'warts and all', as he had said. Charles listened in silence but when she had finished, he said,

'Good grief! That's quite a story. No wonder he's been a bit secretive.'

He took a drink of wine then asked her,

'Did you believe him when he said that the drink and drugs were behind him?'

'I did,' Sophie answered. 'In fact, he seemed completely genuine throughout. When you think about it, why would he be anything else when he had chosen to tell me? He didn't need to say anything, I'd already offered him the money. He could have just accepted it without even speaking to me.'

'That's true,' Charles replied. 'So, I take it that you have given him the money?'

Sophie told him that she had, saying she was thrilled that he said he intended to spend it on a University

Degree course. If he could get in, he wanted to fulfil his ambition of becoming a doctor, she told him.

'Well, that will be amazing if he can achieve it, at his age. I have to say, I am impressed. Of course, you know we will have to be careful where the twins are concerned, don't you?'

'Yes, I know, I've been thinking about that myself. We'll need to keep an eye on that, while still giving him the benefit of the doubt. He certainly seems determined to leave his past behind him.'

'I do love you, you know,' Charles suddenly declared, 'I think you must be the kindest person in the world, Sophie Martin.'

Sophie smiled.

'Early night then?' she said softly.

'Absolutely,' he replied, smiling fondly back at her.

Chapter 14

CELEBRATION

Meanwhile, in his bedsit, John was busy making plans. On Monday he would bank the cheque and send Sophie some flowers as a thank you. He wasn't going to make any sudden changes in his life for the moment, he needed the money to finance his way through University, and he wasn't going to fritter it away. He would carry on working of course but thought he would buy himself a good second-hand car. After that, top of his agenda was to apply to a medical school. He thought that his nursing qualifications and experience he already had, would be enough to gain entry, but he would have to check up on that.

Spending Saturday morning in the library, he compared medical schools and their entry requirements. He definitely wouldn't apply to Bristol. He wanted to explore pastures new. He quite fancied Warwick, as they offered a shortened postgraduate course. He took down the details, determined to ring them up on the following Monday to find out how to apply. He also checked the details of how to get a student loan, which seemed fairly straightforward. As he walked back home from the library, for the first time in years he had a spring in his step. Thanks to his sister, Sophie, he had been given another chance at life. She had placed her trust in him, believed in him, and he wasn't going to let her down.

Now that he had a purpose, he would fill his mind with knowledge he would need in his new life. Dr West sounded good. He knew it may not be as easy as he hoped, his criminal record as a teenager for breaking and entering may prove to be a problem but if he overcame that, he would be on his way at last, and he was determined that nothing would stop him, not even the occasional bout of guilt. He would make amends by saving other lives. That is how he would pay for what he had done. That night, for the first time in ages, he slept soundly. He had still been having the recurring nightmare on and off for months, but it didn't come that night, and he hoped it had gone forever.

Within weeks he had submitted his application to Warwick University Medical School. He had a few nervous moments when he thought they might refuse him because of his criminal record, but some honest discussion at his interview about his efforts over the years to make something of himself, leaving school with no exams but amassing enough qualifications to train to be a nurse and eventually gaining his nursing degree, convinced them that he deserved his opportunity to become a doctor. They offered him an unconditional place, starting in the Autumn of 2014.

He rang Sophie to give her the good news and she was ecstatic for him.

'We need to celebrate!' she exclaimed. 'Why don't you come over for dinner on Saturday?

John hesitated, because he still wasn't sure what Charles thought of him, but Sophie added,

'Oh, do come John, it's such good news, we can't let it pass without some kind of celebration.'

'OK then, of course I'll come. About 6.30 ok?'

'Perfect,' Sophie agreed, 'See you then.'

She hadn't really thought what Charles would say. He hadn't seen much of John since she'd given him the cheque, although she had been in touch with him quite often, encouraging him as he tried to gain a place at medical school. Anyway, she thought, I'm sure he'll be fine about it. After all it's quite an achievement for John, and we should acknowledge it. In fact, when Charles heard that John had been offered an unconditional place at Warwick, he was full of admiration for him and was pleased that Sophie had invited him over.

The children were excited when they knew that John was coming. They hadn't seen him for months, but they still remembered that he'd been happy to play with them, and that was all they needed to know. Henry already had his Lego box on the table, and

Isabella had her favourite jigsaw puzzle at the ready when he arrived.

As it was Saturday and the twins were allowed to stay up late, all the family were to eat together. Sophie thought John might prefer that, missing his own children as he did. They were having beef lasagne which was ready to pop in the oven. In the meantime, Sophie suggested they all go up to the lounge and Charles came in with a bottle of prosecco and three glasses.

'Thought we ought to celebrate properly,' he said, 'That's quite an achievement John, getting into Warwick.'

John smiled and thanked him saying,

'Well, it wasn't easy, I am pretty amazed myself to be honest!'

Sophie had a small parcel in her hands, wrapped in gift paper and tied with a red ribbon.

'Here you are, John, just a little something from Charles and I to say 'well done'. I hope you find it useful.'

John was taken aback. It was so long since anyone had given him a present, he was visibly moved. He opened the parcel to find a Waterman Pen set in black with gold trim. He couldn't speak for a moment. No one had ever, in all his life, given him such a generous and beautiful gift. He hugged Sophie and shook hands with Charles, thanking them profusely.

'You have both been so generous and kind,' he said, 'the way you've made me welcome, accepting me into the family, and sharing the inheritance Sophie, giving me the chance to go to medical school. I am so grateful.'

'Enough of the speeches John, here let's drink a toast to your success.'

Charles opened the prosecco with a pop, to Henry's delight, and poured them all a glass, handing one to John.

'Well, I shouldn't really, but, how can I refuse?'

'To your future,' said Charles, raising his glass.

'Yes, to your future,' Sophie added, smiling broadly 'I look forward to the day we can call you Dr West!'

John thanked them, raised his glass, and said, 'OK, here's to Dr West!'

The whole evening was a great success. John had been touched that they had been determined to make it special for him. He was thrilled with his present. The twins were delightful, and the food was delicious. In fact, it was perfect, apart from one cloud on the horizon.

Will I ever be able to put it out of my mind, he wondered sadly as he drove home. He could sometimes manage to forget about it if he were busy at work or lost in a book. He took it as some kind of a punishment that whenever he was with the person that meant the most to him, the memory of that night was strongest. He knew why of course. Sophie was the one he had hurt the most, but she was the one he loved the most. The fact that she didn't know it was he who was responsible for taking her mother from her didn't help. He knew it and felt guilty and angry with himself for what he'd done. Could he ever make it up to her? He would never be able to be completely honest with her, would he? If only she had found him a couple of months earlier, everything would have been perfect.

Over the next few weeks, John was busy preparing to go to Warwick and didn't see very much of Sophie. It was too difficult for him. She did text him more or less every week, just to see how he was getting on. He still couldn't get used to someone caring about him, but it felt good. A couple of months after the celebratory dinner she rang him to say that Grannie Simons wasn't too well. She'd had a cold that had now turned to a pneumonia and the doctor didn't think she would recover from it. Sophie asked if John would come to visit her, probably for the last time. Given the emotion of the previous meeting, John was reluctant to go, but he knew it would mean a lot to Sophie and so he agreed. They arranged to meet at The Grange the next day.

Grannie Simons was lying in her bed with her eyes closed when they arrived, and they sat down on either side of her. Sophie took her hand and said,

'Hello Grannie, it's Sophie, and John's here to see you as well.'

She opened her eyes and looked at Sophie, and just for a moment there seemed to be a spark of recognition which quickly faded as her mind went off somewhere else. John took hold of her other hand and she looked in his direction. She didn't speak but the look in her eyes said it all. They could tell that once again seeing John had awakened some vestige of memory in her brain. She was remembering her beloved Peter and John was glad he had come.

There didn't seem much point in speaking and they both sat in a companiable silence. It seemed enough somehow, just to share this short, final time with Grannie. Her breathing was shallow and laboured and it was obvious that she was very poorly. After about half an hour she had fallen asleep. One of the carers came in to check on her.

'She's sleeping most of the time now,' she said quietly to Sophie, 'she will probably fade gently away. We'll just keep her comfortable and let you know if there's any change.'

Sophie thanked her and she and John got up to leave. Sophie kissed Grannie gently on her forehead and John, surprisingly, did the same, while in his head, he was saying 'I'm so sorry Grannie.'

As they walked out of The Grange and over to their cars, Sophie asked John if he fancied a coffee some-where, but John had felt the guilt particularly badly, sitting with Grannie Simons, and he needed to find some respite. Being with Sophie just made it worse, so he said he was sorry, but he had to get ready for his shift. She was obviously disappointed but said that she understood and thanked him for coming anyway. With that, they hugged briefly then got into their cars and went their separate ways.

Sadly, Grannie passed away peacefully a week later, and Sophie rang John to let him know. The funeral was at the end of the following week and John felt that he should attend. Sophie would be hurt if he didn't. There were thankfully few people at the crematorium at Holy Soul's Cemetery on Bath Road, just Charles and Sophie, a few old friends of Grannie's, and a couple of members of staff from The Grange, no one who needed an introduction to John, which suited him fine. Sophie asked him if he would come along to the house for some lunch afterwards, but he said he had taken a couple of hours off work to come and had to get back as soon as possible. He hated seeing the disappointment on Sophie's face once again, but he couldn't cope with the guilt being with her generated and left immediately after the crematorium service.

September came round quickly, and John had managed to find himself a room in a flat share with three other medical students in Leamington Spa. He settled in well, although it seemed to take a long while to get round to anything 'medical', what with 'getting to know you' events and fresher's activities, but finally he was able to get down to some serious study. He supposed his fellow housemates found him a bit stand-offish, but he wasn't much interested in socialising. It had taken him long enough to get there and he was determined not to waste a minute of his time at medical school.

Chapter 15

LIFE GOES ON

Getting to know John and hearing about his life had rather woken Sophie's social conscience. She now understood only too well, that not everyone had the kind of life she'd had. She was awakened to the fact that there was great need, even in a place as affluent as Bath. She volunteered to help out at the Foodbank and had her eyes opened to the level of poverty in the city. She did a couple of sessions a week and was touched, not only by the gratitude of the people receiving help, but also by the generosity of the people of Bath who donated the food and other items to help perfect strangers.

Sophie had also been thinking about her own future recently. Inspired, she supposed ,by John's determination to follow his dream, she began to feel that now the children were getting older and a little more independent, she would like to re-embark on her own career.

After leaving Uni with a 2.1 in History, she had decided that a teaching career would suit her very well, and had taken a post graduate teacher training course. She embarked on her first year, teaching history at a secondary school in Bristol. Charles was working at the same school and within two years they were married, and she was pregnant with the twins. Although pleased she was expecting twins, she secretly admitted to herself that she was disappointed she had to give up her career before it had really begun. She did consider whether to carry on working and send the children to nursery, but Charles was adamant that he wanted her to stay at home, for a few years anyway. There would be plenty of time, he told her, for her to take up a teaching career once they were less dependent on her.

In the end, she had accepted it and indeed, had thrown herself one hundred percent into building a home for them all and nurturing her children. However, seeing John grab the opportunity to achieve his lifetime's ambition, she felt that now was her time. She said as much to Charles one evening, after the children had gone up to bed. At first, he seemed a little ambivalent about it. Of course it would make life a bit more complicated for him. He had a responsible job and having Sophie at home, supporting him and organising his life had suited him very well. However, he knew that she had given up her career all those years ago to concentrate on looking after their growing family. At the back of his mind, he also knew that being the person she was, Sophie wouldn't be satisfied indefinitely with being a 'stay at home mum'.

They therefore agreed she would start to look for a part time teaching post, somewhere nearby, that she could work in with childcare. As it happened, it was too late to apply for the current academic year's intake, and she placed herself on the supply teaching register. Within a month or so, she was offered a few hours teaching history at the local comprehensive. It meant a lot of hard work, catching up with the syllabus, which had changed substantially since she had taught anyone. There would be quite a bit of adjusting to be done in the Martin household, with everyone expected to start helping out with the household chores. They discussed it with the children and they agreed that they would of course help mummy. Between them they decided to take turns at loading and emptying the dishwasher. All very amicable, but Sophie wondered how long that would last!

It was hard work, but as she did in all things, Sophie threw herself into it with total commitment, and within a month or two things had settled down to some sort of routine. The work was a bit erratic of course, being supply teaching, and she was determined to find a permanent post for the next academic year.

She did in fact find a part time but permanent

position at the local comprehensive, teaching History and English to ages ten to thirteen. As she was now earning a decent salary, the family finances were sound, and with money in the bank inherited from her mother, she and Charles decided to send the twins to a private school and they were thriving in every way. Sophie never tired of telling them how lucky they were and tried to instil a social conscience in them by involving them whenever she was helping out at a food collection for the food bank outside the supermarket. She supposed this was her way of assuaging the hint of guilt she still felt when she thought about John and compared his life to her own.

Sophie and John didn't see much of each other over the next few years although they kept in touch regularly by text and email. Sophie eagerly followed his progress through his years at Warwick, and was always happy to hear his news. For his part, he was happy that she was always interested in how he was getting on, offering praise when he did well, and encouragement if he was struggling, which actually wasn't often. He knew he had found his niche in life and was looking forward to graduating so that his life in medicine could truly begin.

John found he was able to push the events of 'that night' as he thought of it, to the back of his mind. Gradually he began to rationalise it. He convinced himself he'd had no choice. He could not have lived with that second and final rejection by his birth mother. It would have destroyed him, literally, so it had been a matter of self preservation, doing what he did. Most of the time, he was fine with it. However, whenever he was with Sophie it wasn't so easy. He knew she still missed her mother; she often said so. In those moments the guilt reared up again and the pain he had inflicted on her, the sister who was his only blood relative, who had been so kind and generous to him, echoed in his own heart. Consequently, he largely avoided being in Sophie's company, contenting himself with communicating through emails and texts.

He did join the family at the cottage in Yorkshire a couple of times and it was lovely for him to catch up with Henry and Isabella and to watch them growing up. Of course, that always brought memories of James and Abigail, but he comforted himself with the thought that once he was qualified he would certainly visit Australia and find them again. He was sure they would be proud of what he'd achieved and he would be in a position financially to start being a real dad to them once again, and maybe help them through their education one day too.

The years rolled by and Sophie was happy. She was doing a job she loved, Charles was doing well at school, the children were strong and healthy and she was proud of John's achievements, happy that she'd been able to have a hand in facilitating them. She was thrilled when he called her to tell her he'd gained a First Class Degree and asked whether she and Charles would be able to come to his graduation ceremony in a few weeks time. Of course, she readily accepted, saying she wouldn't miss it for the world.

Chapter 16

GRADUATION

July 2018

The day had finally arrived. The day John West would become Dr John West. As he filed into the hall with his fellow students, he scanned the assembled parents for Sophie and Charles. He knew they would be there. If it hadn't been for Sophie, he would never have achieved his lifelong ambition. As he walked down the aisle towards the front of the hall, he glanced back at the balcony and was thrilled to see them there. He wasn't surprised Sophie had managed to end up in the front row. She would have made sure they arrived in plenty of time, determined to get a good view of his graduation.

Sophie, what a wonderful sister she had turned out to be, he thought to himself. If she hadn't shared her inheritance with him, even though she didn't have to, he would never have had the chance to become a doctor, which is all he had ever wanted. John took his seat among the other graduands. As he waited for the ceremony to begin, he reflected over the last five years.

It had been a long road. Initially, he had feared he wouldn't be accepted. Indeed, he had to work hard to convince the University, and himself, that his criminal career began and ended while he was still a troubled teenager, and that since then, he had been a law-abiding citizen. In the end, they accepted his submission and agreed that his nursing experience and degree were sufficient for him to study medicine at Warwick University on a four-year course.

The work had been hard of course, but because of his passion and dedication he'd applied himself a hundred percent to his studies and achieved excellent results. In fact, he had been awarded a first-class honours degree. He stood out among the younger students whose main aims seemed to be to make the most of the social life being a university student had to offer. He wasn't interested in any of that, being determined to do himself and Sophie proud. He had made some friends, of course, but none that he would call close. He still maintained a certain distance from people, with the exception of Sophie, because of the terrible secret he still carried. The memory had faded over the years, as his determination to do good in the world, and his knowledge of how he could achieve that, grew stronger. But it was still there, and he knew it would never completely go away. Now he must prepare to say the Oath in a few minutes time, in front of his peers and their families. It would be hard, but he swore to himself that he would be true to it from this point onwards until the day he died.

After several minutes, the dignitaries filed into the hall, led by the Chancellor of the University. Among them were the lecturers and professors who had supported and guided the students through their long years of study. Although this was of necessity a solemn occasion, the Chancellor was determined that it would be one of celebration too and set the tone immediately by asking the graduands to applaud their families, thanking them for the support they had given them. They all stood and faced their guests, applauding loudly. John was smiling broadly and clapping enthusiastically as he turned towards the balcony and caught Sophie's eye. She was beaming and nodded her head in acknowledgement. Sophie's eyes moistened with pride as she looked at John. He had come so far. It was just a shame that mum couldn't be here to witness this, she thought to herself.

After the usual speeches, one by one, the graduands were called up to receive their degrees and eventually it was John's turn. He strode proudly up the steps on to the platform where the Chancellor handed him his degree certificate. He turned towards the audience who were clapping loudly and, smiling broadly, looked up at Sophie, holding up his certificate in triumph, then walked off the stage to take his seat among his fellow graduates. When all the certificates had been presented, there was another round of applause after which the newly graduated doctors were asked to read the oath out loud together. John read it with the utmost sincerity, determined to uphold every tenet of it in the years ahead. It was an emotional moment for him.

They were then declared to be fully qualified doctors, at which point a tremendous cheer went up followed by tumultuous applause and a standing ovation lasting fully two minutes. John, along with his fellow graduates was elated.

The whole day was magical for John, but also for Sophie, and even for Charles, who had to admit to feeling immense admiration for what John had achieved, and actually told him so, much to John's surprise. He had never been sure what Charles thought of him. Now he invited John to join them for lunch before they set off back to Bath, and he was happy to accept. He thanked them for coming and said, once again, that without their support he could never have achieved his dream of becoming a doctor.

After the official group photo had been taken, Charles took some with his phone, and one of the young doctors offered to take one of the three of them. Finally, they went off to find somewhere to eat, ending up at a promising looking Italian restaurant where they enjoyed authentic pizzas and salad. Sophie knew John had been undecided whether to stay in Warwick and apply for a post as a Junior Doctor there, or to move back to Somerset, and now she asked him what he had decided to do. He told her that for the moment he was waiting to hear from a hospital in Swindon. He had applied for a Junior Doctor post. The lease on his flat in Leamington Spa was due to expire at the end of August, so he had plenty of time to find something in Swindon if his application was success-ful. Sophie told him she was glad he wouldn't be too far away and hoped they would see more of him in the future.

John walked them back to their car from the res-taurant and, giving Sophie a hug and shaking hands with Charles, he said goodbye, promising to keep in touch regularly.

Sophie and Charles were on the M40 heading south by three thirty. The twins would be home from school by the time they arrived. They were growing up fast now. At fourteen years old they were quite capable of finding themselves something to eat but were still prone to squabbling and Sophie didn't like to leave them alone for too long. They should easily be home by five thirty, Charles thought.

'That was a lovely day,' Sophie reflected. 'You know, I felt so proud of John and what he's achieved, and I know that mum would have too.'

'Of course, she would,' Charles agreed.

'Do you know,' he went on, 'it won't be long before Henry and Isabella will be up on a stage somewhere, receiving their degrees, and what a proud day that will be.'

'Don't,' Sophie pleaded, 'I don't want them to grow up so fast. I want to enjoy them for a bit longer yet.'

'I know, I just meant that time goes so fast. I can't believe it's six years since your mother died and we met John. What a turn up that was.'

'It was, and how strange that it took mum's death to bring John and I together. It's odd how things work out sometimes,' she said, without knowing just how true that was.

Chapter 17

ACCEPTANCE?

Graduation day had been wonderful for John. The pinnacle of all his ambitions, and the fact that Sophie was there to witness him receiving his degree made it even more special.

He received a letter from the Swindon Hospital Trust the following week offering him a Junior Doctor contract, starting on the first of October. He was thrilled. Finally, he would be a real doctor with real patients, and he would be able to start making a difference to people's lives.

He began to prepare for leaving Leamington Spa and started searching for somewhere to live in Swindon. Having lived fairly frugally over the four years he'd spent at Warwick, he still had enough of his inheritance left to put down on a part share of a small two bedroomed house on a pleasant, new estate on the outskirts of Swindon. The purchase went through quickly and by the beginning of September he had the keys to his new home. It was a proud moment when he put his keys in the lock for the first time. The kitchen was fully fitted, and he quickly furnished the rest of the house with essentials, moving in during the second week of September.

Since his graduation day though, he had been giving a lot of thought to quite a different matter. Was it possible, he wondered, he could make things right with Sophie once and for all? He loved her dearly and wanted to be as close to her as any brother should be to his sister, but always there was that invisible barrier between them. Every fibre of his being was calling out to him to confess to her what he'd done. Surely, after all these years of seeing him work so hard to make something of himself, there was a chance that she could forgive him.

Could he make her understand why he did it if he told her how her mother had rejected him all over again. Would she see that, at that point in his life, he had needed more than anything, the love and acceptance she should have given him, not to be sent away. Would she see how intolerable that had been for him, given his state of mind at the time? After weeks of deliberation, he finally convinced himself that she would, and decided that he needed to go to Bath and have that conversation with her as soon as possible.

Although Sophie and John had kept in touch by text every couple of weeks, it was one morning in September when he finally rang her. He said he would like to come over to Bath one day soon as he had something to tell her but would prefer to see her alone. She was intrigued but said she would love to see him. The children and Charles had just started back at school, so any weekday would be fine she said, and invited him to come for lunch. They agreed that he would come the following Tuesday. Sophie said she would love to hear about his new house and all about the job he was due to start in October.

Even as he was driving over to Bath, he still wasn't completely sure whether he would have the courage to tell her about her mother. How would she react? Then he thought – this is Sophie we're talking about. Kind, generous, empathic Sophie. He was sure she would understand and that was all he wanted from her. Not once did it occur to him to ask himself what she might do with the information he was planning to give her. He had lived with what he'd done for so long that he had rationalised it, accepted it as something he'd had to do, and was convinced that he could make Sophie do the same. All he could think about was how, once this barrier was dismantled, he and Sophie could have a proper brother and sister relationship.

Nonetheless he had to confess to feeling rather nervous as he knocked on Sophie's door.

'Good afternoon, Dr West,' she said with a smile as she opened the door. She welcomed him in with a hug and a peck on the cheek. John never failed to be amazed at how warm and loving she was. She said she was just preparing lunch and they should go down into the kitchen. He could talk to her while she got on with it.

John followed her down the stairs, wondering when he should actually broach the subject he'd come to talk to her about. He sat down on a stool at the island workbench in the kitchen while Sophie was cutting up vegetables.

They chatted about his house and his new job. He showed Sophie a picture of the house which he had on his phone and she said she was thrilled for him, that at last he would have his own place. She asked about his job at Swindon and he explained that as a Junior Doctor he would be rotating round various departments for a while, gaining more experience. Then they had discussed the twins and how they were getting on at school and what options they had chosen for their GCSE's.

Finally, Sophie asked him what it was that he had wanted to talk to her about.

John paused, still unsure if this was the right thing to do. Then he thought of everything he had gone through to get to this point in his life, but he realised that to be truly free to move forward, he had to clear his conscience as far as Sophie was concerned. He would have to tell her. If he couldn't, there would always be a barrier between them.

'Well, it's not easy, but I have to be honest with you Sophie, if we are to be truly close as brother and sister.'

Sophie was a little taken aback at this.

'So, have you not been honest with me John?' she asked, with a frown.

'Not entirely,' he went on, 'I have to tell you that I had already met our mother before you came to find me.'

Sophie took a step back and put down the knife she had been using.

'What?' she murmured, 'What do you mean John? When? How?'

He explained that after he'd lost Julie and his children, and the job he loved, he'd been at such a low point in his life he had come to believe that the disastrous course his life had taken had really stemmed from the point at which his birth mother had given him away. He had realised, he told Sophie, that he needed to find her to ask her why she had done it. He had also fervently hoped that she would now want to have him back in her life and to make amends for the life to which she had condemned him.

At this point, Sophie, was beginning to feel a little defensive on behalf of her mother, saying,

'But John, she had no way of knowing what kind of life you would have, did she?'

'Exactly!' John went on, 'All the more reason for her not to give me away!'

Sophie said nothing, unable to disagree with the logic of his argument.

He went on to tell her how he had gained access to his adoption records and found out who his mother was, eventually finding her address. He decided to go to see her.

'John, surely you didn't just turn up?' Sophie asked incredulously.

'I did,' he replied. 'I couldn't risk her refusing to see me you see. So, yes, I did literally just knock on her door.'

'When was this?' Sophie asked.

'It was at the end of April,' he told her.

'So that was just before I took her to the doctor's. So, what happened? She never said anything to me about you coming to see her.'

He told her how devastated he had been when she had made it clear that she wanted nothing to do with him. He had come to her in his hour of greatest need, at the lowest point in his miserable existence and she hadn't wanted to know him.

'John, I'm so sorry,' Sophie murmured, 'That must have been horrible for you. I imagine it was because she had never told any of us about you and it had come as quite a shock, you turning up out of the blue like that. What a pity you couldn't have found me first.'

'I know, Sophie, I wish I had, more than you'll ever know.'

'So why didn't you tell me about all this when we met in Bristol that day.'

'Because that's not the end of the story.'

He paused and Sophie asked him what he meant.

'Well, that wasn't the last time I saw her. I saw her again three weeks later.'

He paused again to let Sophie digest that.

'But three weeks later she was in hospital, having her operation.'

'Yes,' he agreed. 'I was on the night shift that night and I saw her in the side ward.'

'Did you speak to her?' Sophie demanded.

'No, she was asleep.'

'So, you must have known she died that night. It must have been the talk of the department, as no one knew how or why it happened.'

'I did know that she died Sophie, because ...'

Suddenly Sophie realised what he was trying to tell her.

'Oh my God!' she exclaimed, 'It was you! You killed her!'

'Sophie! You've got to understand. Right then it seemed to me that every ghastly thing that had happened to me in my life was her fault. She had given me away, and finally, when I went to her in desperation, she had rejected me again.'

Sophie was staring at him in horror, unable to comprehend the magnitude of what he was saying.

'But how?' she managed, 'The post-mortem showed nothing.'

He just uttered the word 'insulin' and finally, she understood.

'But Sophie, I've made amends. I'm a doctor now and I'm going to save lives. I've worked so hard to get to this point and all I want is to do good in the world. Please, you must forgive me.'

'Forgive you!' she screamed at him. 'You've just told me that you killed my mother, and you ask me to forgive you. I'll never forgive you!'

She picked up her phone and turned it on.

'What are you doing Sophie?' he asked in a cold, now calm voice.

'I'm ringing the police, of course.'

'Sophie, put the phone down,' he said menacingly. 'I can't let you do that.'

Sophie carried on dialling. He lunged forward trying to snatch the phone from her, but she put it behind her back to stop him getting hold of it. He let out an unearthly wail which seemed to come from the bottom of his soul and grabbed her around her neck.

'Why couldn't you understand!' he screamed at her as he continued to squeeze her throat.

Sophie was flailing around, trying to escape his grip, when her fingers felt the handle of the knife she'd been using. She managed to pick it up and swung it in an arc towards him feeling the sickening squelch as it entered his flesh. Suddenly, he let go of his grip on her throat as he clutched the side of his neck, trying to stem the blood that was spurting out in all directions..

Sophie staggered away from him coughing and spluttering as she tried to catch her breath. She watched in horror as John, still trying to stem the flow of blood from his neck, slid to the floor. He knew perfectly well what was happening to him. He was a doctor, after all.

The last words he spoke were,

'Sophie, forgive me.'

The police arrived ten minutes later. The door was locked, and they had to force their way in. They found a scene of utter carnage in the kitchen and Sophie, covered in blood, sitting in the garden gazing out over the city.

She had managed to dial 999 and give them her address, telling them that she had just killed her brother. After that, her brain had seemed to shut down and all she wanted to do was to sit quietly and wait for someone, anyone, to come and take charge.

Chapter 18

AN EPILOGUE

Sophie felt the cool grass between her toes and the gentle breeze caressing her upturned face, her eyes closed against the glare of the summer sun. Hugging her knees to her chest, she opened her eyes to look down on the wonderful scene before her. She never tired of this view of the city.

Gradually, she became aware of a distant tapping sound and wondered what it could be. It grew more insistent, until she could ignore it no longer and opened her eyes, finding herself staring at the white walls of the tiny room where she had existed for months, escaping its confines only in her dreams. The tapping was coming from the radiator and had become louder now, no doubt some poor creature who had no other way of telling anyone of the anguish she was feeling.

Sophie looked up at the tiny square of sky that masqueraded as a window, but through which sunshine never penetrated. Today though, she would see the sun. Today she was being released back into the world. She would soon be back home, able to hug her children for the first time in eighteen months, and Charles too, of course. He had been wonderful through all of this. She suspected he blamed himself for allowing John to come into their lives. In truth, of course, he could not have stopped it. The need for her to find her brother once she knew of his existence, and his need for a family to belong to, were too strong.

Sophie had had plenty of time to think about what had led her to this situation. Her feelings about John had crystallised into something akin to pity. Of course, she did feel guilty for wielding the knife, but she knew she'd had no choice. In his anguish at experiencing yet another rejection, and the prospect of the destruction of his future once more as she had tried to ring the police, had been too much for his mind to take.

She knew she could have handled it better. If she had been able to disguise her shock and keep things calmer, not trying to immediately contact the police, he wouldn't have attacked her. In reality, that scenario was impossible. She was, of course, shocked to be told by this man who she had grown to love and admire, that he had actually killed her mother. He should have known that she would be horrified. She supposed, he had over the years, rationalised what he had done as being a necessity, given his state of mind at the time, but surely, he couldn't have expected her to accept it and do nothing with the information?

Well, she would never know. John was gone, and what a waste of a life it had been. All that effort, repeatedly climbing back out of despair to finally make something of himself, only for it to end like that. If her mother hadn't rejected him for a second time, if he hadn't done what he'd done, and then, if she hadn't stumbled across the shoebox and been determined to find him, the events of that dreadful day would never have happened.

Sophie had little recollection of what had happened immediately afterwards. She had been taken to the police station and questioned for several hours by the police. The house was a crime scene and the family moved into an hotel while forensics were dealt with. She had been on bail for several months until her trial, at which she was horrified to be sentenced to three years for manslaughter with the mitigating plea of self-defence. Now, after serving eighteen months, she had been given parole and today would sit in her garden once more. She was content.

As for John, his body had been taken away by the police and a post-mortem carried out, after which he had been cremated without ceremony, and without anyone who cared about him there to witness it. A month after leaving prison, however, Sophie made her way to the crematorium, laying flowers in the Garden of Remembrance, bearing a label on which she had written,

'In memory of my brother, Dr John West. Rest in Peace, John. With love from your sister, Sophie.'

END

About the Author

Marilyn Freeman enjoyed a rather varied career pathway, including starting out as an industrial chemist and progressing into entrepreneurship, manufacturing toiletry products among other things. She is also a trained bereavement counsellor. She has been married twice and lived in various places around the UK and also spent several eventful years living in Lagos, Nigeria in the 1970's. Since retiring from industry she has spent several years editing and self-publishing books for her husband, and writing and creating life-story and poetry books for various private clients. She also has twenty grandchildren and five great grandchildren which also keep her rather busy!

She enjoys writing about people and the interactions of differing personalities. She loves to take a long look at the lives of her characters and is fascinated by the way apparently simple decisions can cause effects that resonate across generations, sometimes with devastating results.

If you would like to know more about Marilyn, visit her web page at www.spellbrooktales.com

Other books by Marilyn Freeman

Marilyn Freeman's book, **Karma; A Mystery in Paris** tells the story of Adrienne, age 22, as she embarks on a journey to Paris to discover what happened to her mother who left the family home ten years previously and never returned. Adrienne uncovers a story spanning three decades and having its roots in the Nazi occupation of Paris in the 1940's. With courage and determination Adrienne pursues the truth and finally gets her answers, but there are many twists and turns along the way, finally reaching a shocking climax.

Ebook and paperback editions of **Karma: A Mystery in Paris** are available from most retailers.

The ebook edition of **Secrets and Lives** is available from most book retailers.

Connect with Marilyn Freeman

Email inbox@marilynfreeman.org
Web site: http://www.spellbrooktales.com
Facebook: www.facebook.com/marilynswriting
Twitter: www.twitter.com/marilynswriting
Instagram:www.instagram.com/marilyn.freeman.11

Discussion Guide

I hope you enjoyed reading Secrets and Lives. Here are some suggestions for you to use as a discussion guide within your reading group:

How did SECRETS AND LIVES make you feel?

How do you feel about how the story was told?

What did you think about the main characters?

Did the characters seem believable to you? Did they remind you of anyone?

If you were making a movie of this book, who would you cast?

Which parts of SECRETS AND LIVES stood out to you?

Would you read another book by this author? Why or why not?

If you got the chance to ask the author of this book one question, what would it be?

What do you think of the book's title? How does it relate to the book's contents? What other title might you choose?

What did you think about the ending?

What themes did you detect in SECRETS AND LIVES?

What is your impression of the author?

Thank you for reading SECRETS AND LIVES and for taking the trouble to discuss it within your group.